Menagerie

Menagerie

Kristy Tate

Indie Artist Press | Brackettville, Texas

Menagerie
A novel by Kristy Tate
First Paperback Edition
Copyright © Kristy Tate 2018
All Rights Reserved
Printed in the United States of America
ISBN-13:978-1-62522-121-6

Publisher Information
Indie Artist Press
P. O. Box 131
Brackettville, TX 78832
www.indieartistpress.com

From Declan's Research
Animism (from Latin anima, "breath, spirit, life") is
the worldview that non-human entities
—such as animals, plants, and inanimate objects—
possess a spiritual essence.

Chapter One

The birds heralded the storm, as they always did. They liked to be the bearers of scuttlebutt. Although, as Lizbet had learned long ago, not all birds were created equal, and some species were much more reliable than others. Not that they lied, very few creatures had the ability or cunning, but rather in their haste to be the first in the know, some blurted out misconceptions and half-truths.

Not that Lizbet had much familiarity with liars—or people, in general—but she'd read of several, as Rose, her mother, had accumulated an impressive library over the years. Not that Lizbet was in any position to know what was and was not impressive library-wise, or any otherwise, since Lizbet herself had never been off the island she and Rose called home.

The howling wind drowned out the calls of birds, and the chatter of squirrels and chipmunks. Opossum, skunks, and fox sought shelter in the forest's thickets. Rats and mice scurried to find hidey-holes. Lizbet fetched an armful of wood from the shed to stoke the fire while her mother gathered candles.

Wind rustled the tarp protecting the woodpile. The pine trees, used to standing straight and tall, moaned as the wind whipped through their canopy, and bent them in directions they didn't wish to go.

"A man approaches," Wordsworth whined, terror tainting his words.

Lizbet looked over the German Shepherd's furry head to the storm-tossed sea. The Sound, normally a tranquil gray-blue slate, roiled as if shaken by an invisible hand. Lizbet couldn't see anyone, but her heart quickened. "Are you sure?" She saw nothing but a curtain of rain, an angry sky, and churning tide. The gulls, who generally swooped above the bay, had wisely found shelter. The otters, too, had disappeared, and for once the noisy, boisterous sea lions, were silent.

The dog nodded. *"He's lost, but hopeful."*

"Hopeful? Of what?"

Wordsworth shook his head. When another flash of lightening lit the sky, his ears flattened and his tail drooped and he cowered as the thunder boomed.

"Come," Lizbet said, "let's go inside. Only an idiot would be out on the water today."

"He's no longer on the water," Wordsworth whined again. *"His boat has landed."*

Lizbet peered into the storm, saw nothing more than before, and added another log to her collection. Their cottage was made of stone, but the adjacent shed which housed the woodpile, gardening tools, and bird seed, was constructed of recycled wood. Wind blew through the slats and rattled the shake roof. The cottage would be warm and dry in a way the shed never could.

Wordsworth whimpered again. Lizbet knew he longed for the comforts of the house as much as she did, but she also understood he had an important job to do, and he would never back away from protecting her and her mother from strangers.

"There's no one there," Lizbet said, stomping toward the cottage. She climbed the steps and pulled open the Dutch door. The warm comforting scent of the crackling fire mingled with the aroma of ginger cookies welcomed her in.

Rose stood at a large pine table, stacking the cookies onto a plate. Lizbet stared at the number of cookies, knowing that she and her mother would never be able to eat so many. Her mother was waif-thin with flyaway blond hair as insubstantial as her slender frame.

"There's a man in the cove," Lizbet said, wondering if her mother already knew, and if so, why she hadn't warned her.

Rose kept her gaze focused on the cookies and blushed the color of her namesake. She was as fair as Lizbet was dark. *We are as night and day*, her mother would say, *Together, we are all we need.*

"Are you expecting someone?" Lizbet demanded.

"No, not really, but I..." Rose's voice trailed away.

Lizbet clomped through the kitchen to the living room, weaving through the stacks of books to the fireplace. She dropped her logs onto the hearth, placed her hands on her hips, and marched back into the kitchen. She hated surprises, but she was also curious.

"Who is this man?" Not Leonard, the postman—her mother would never blush for the potato-shaped letter carrier. Besides, Leonard would never venture to the island in a storm. He only came every other Tuesday. Today was Saturday.

"You don't need to worry about him," Rose said without meeting Lizbet's eye.

"Why is he coming? Will he bring books?"

Rose laughed, but it sounded strange—strained and nervous. Lizbet decided that she already disliked this man. She plucked a cookie off the plate.

Rose looked up sharply, an expectant look on her face.

Lizbet contemplated her cookie, suddenly suspicious. Her mother studied and experimented with herbs and she'd taught Lizbet a variety of recipes. Dandelions to

lighten the mood, lavender to soothe worries, chamomile to bring sleep, basil to stimulate energy, and ginger root to make one forget. Lizbet sniffed the cookie and touched it with her tongue.

Her mother watched.

Lizbet smiled, took a big bite and left the kitchen. In the privacy of her own room, she went to the window and pulled it open. A cold breeze flew in, ruffling the drapes, and blowing about the papers on her desk. Ignoring the wind, Lizbet stuck her head outside and spat the cookie out into the storm. She slammed the window closed.

"What are you doing?" Rose asked.

Lizbet started. She hadn't heard her mother come in. Wrapping her arms around herself, Lizbet said, "I was looking for the man."

Rose's lips lifted into a smile. "Please don't worry about him. Here, I've brought you some tea." She set down a steaming mug on Lizbet's bedside table. "Ginger root, your favorite."

"Thanks."

"Want to come and read by the fire?" Rose asked.

Lizbet glanced back at the storm on the other side of the window. An idea tickled in the back of her mind. "In a second," she said. After plopping down on her bed, Lizbet sipped from the mug, but she didn't swallow. Instead, she let the tea warm her tongue.

Rose lifted her own mug to her lips and watched Lizbet. Lizbet set the mug back down and met her mother's gaze. After an awkward moment, Rose lifted her shoulder in a halfhearted shrug and headed down the hall.

Lizbet bounced from the bed, closed the door, and spat the tea back into the mug. She poured the entire cup out the window and climbed back onto her bed. She lay perfectly still, waiting for her mom to re-enter the room. She didn't have to wait long.

A few moments later, her bedroom door creaked open. With her eyes firmly closed, Lizbet practiced her corpse pose and didn't even flinch as she heard her mother steal into the room. Rose tucked a quilt around Lizbet's shoulders before creeping back out and closing the door with a whisper click.

Lizbet peeked open an eye and met Wordsworth's steady, brown-eyed gaze. "Who is he?"

"I don't know," the dog whimpered, *"but he isn't scared."*

"How can you tell?" Lizbet asked.

"The smell. All emotions have a smell."

"My mom—what's her smell?"

Wordsworth jumped up on the bed beside Lizbet and nestled against her. *"She loves you."*

"I know. But I don't know what that has to do with anything."

Wordsworth whimpered again and snuggled closer. *"You have to let me out so I can meet this man."*

"I can't. If I do, she'll know I'm awake. You're on your own."

Wordsworth blew out a breath, stood, shook himself, and jumped down. He went to the door to bark and whine. It didn't do any good. Her mother ignored him, which told Lizbet two things. One: the potion Rose had given Lizbet must have been so strong that Rose didn't worry about Wordsworth waking her. Two: Rose didn't want to be interrupted.

Lizbet sat up as a thought assaulted her.

Wordsworth, as if reading her mind, jumped back up beside her and gazed into her eyes.

"This man is my father!" Lizbet blurted out.

"You cannot know this," Wordsworth whimpered.

"She loves him enough to drug me just to spend time with him! Of course he's my father!"

Wordsworth moaned a disagreement.

Lizbet had a lot of questions—mostly because she lived a solitary life with her mother on an uninhabited island in the Puget Sound. She had faith that all of her questions would eventually be answered, but the biggest questions in her heart and mind all centered around her father.

Lizbet kicked off the quilt and crawled off the bed.

Wordsworth placed his nose against her thigh, stopping her. *"There must be a good reason your mother doesn't want you to meet this man."*

"She never said she didn't want me to meet him."

Wordsworth snorted. *"If she had wanted you to meet him, she wouldn't have given you the ginger root tea."*

Suddenly Lizbet hated her mother. "She can't keep me from my own father."

Wordsworth parked his butt against the door like a giant hairy roadblock. *"You do not know he is your father."*

"Of course he is. Who else could he be? Now move." She grabbed Wordsworth's collar to pull him away. His fur bunched up around his collar, but he wouldn't budge.

Lizbet tried the doorknob, but since Wordsworth outweighed her by nearly fifty pounds the door wouldn't open. Lizbet flounced to the window.

"Where are you going?" Wordsworth asked, his ears poking toward the ceiling.

"To meet my dad." Lizbet threw open the window. The wind spat rain in her face and carried a breath of bone-chilling cold into the room.

Wordsworth stood and shook himself, but didn't move away from the door.

Lizbet had one leg thrown over the sill, and her exposed foot was already soaking from the storm.

"You'll look like a drowned cat if you go outside," Wordsworth said.

She sent him a dirty look. He gazed back at her. She clambered out the window. The rain hit her like hundreds of shards of ice. The cold stung her face and pierced her clothes. She ran around to the side of the house so she could look in the windows.

Inside, sitting side by side on the sofa amongst the towers of books, snuggled together in front of the fire was

her mom and a man. Lizbet knew she'd never seen him before—not that she could remember, at least—but there was something in her that recognized him. She felt as drawn to him as a bird to a worm.

But as she watched him laughing with her mother, Lizbet had another realization. She knew that even if she introduced herself to this man, because of the cookies on the platter, in time, he would never remember her. She'd only be a vague recollection—a face he couldn't place.

Lizbet never drank ginger root tea again.

Chapter Two

In mid-April, when the crocuses began to lift their heads from the ground and the daffodils unfurled toward the bleak but not yet warm sun, a pod of gray whales splashed past the western side of the island. Lizbet loved this time of year when the plants and animals roused themselves from winter's frozen grasp. The garden, still crusty with ice, yielded beneath Lizbet's hoe as she worked compost into the soil. Lizbet longed to be out in the dinghy to hear of the whales' southern adventures, but Rose kept her in the garden.

Lizbet slid her mother a glance. Beneath the enormous straw hat Rose always wore, a worry line etched between her eyebrows, and her lips pulled into a thin, straight line. Tension radiated from her, and Lizbet felt powerless against it.

Lizbet tried restating her argument. "I know a man came last night. What I don't know is why you insist on lying about it."

"This is not up for discussion," Rose said.

"How can—" her words faded away when she caught sight of Wordsworth flicking his ears, something he did when stressed. He sat at the garden's edge, his ears pricked, his eyes vigilant, despite the cataracts clouding his vision.

Tennyson, an orange tabby, perched in the branches of the maple tree, twitching his tail and complaining about the birds swooping around him.

"A man comes," Wordsworth whimpered.

Lizbet braced against her hoe and glanced out at the tranquil bay. Wispy clouds trailed across the robin's egg blue sky. She couldn't see an approaching boat. She moved to the furthest edge of the garden, out of her mother's earshot. "Is it him again?" she whispered to Wordsworth.

"No. Someone else."

"The postman?"

"No."

Lizbet resumed hoeing when she caught her mother's gaze on her. She'd learned long ago that her mother couldn't hear or understand the animals the way she did. At first, this had bothered her. For years, she had believed her mother to be all-knowing and all-powerful, but in time, Lizbet had grown to love that she had an ability her mother

not only didn't share but also discounted as a childish whim akin to make-believe friends and monsters beneath the bed.

"The whales dislike him. His boat is loud and he's disrupting their path."

Lizbet frowned against the sun.

"Tired already?" Rose called out without looking up from her work.

"No, I thought I heard an engine."

Rose's head jerked over her shoulder and her spine stiffened. She cocked her head, listening.

Gulls cried out as they wheeled overhead. *"A man, a man, a man."*

"I don't hear anything," Rose said slowly, resuming her hoeing.

"A large boat, yet manned alone," Wordsworth said.

"Not quite," Tennyson said, twitching his whiskers as he lounged in a nearby apple tree. The tree's pink blossoms offset his orange fur and Lizbet wondered if the cat knew this. He was so vain she thought he might. *"He brings a creature."*

Creature was Tennyson's word for dog.

Wordsworth's ears pricked up. *"I cannot smell him."*

"Nor I, but the albatross spotted him," Tennyson said. *"He's wolfish."*

Wordsworth began to pace along the garden's edge.

Rose lifted her face to the sun. Lizbet saw the questions in her mother's sapphire eyes, but she didn't know the answers. She wasn't even sure of the questions.

"There's something I need to tell you, pet," Rose began, drawing near. "Not just one thing, actually..." She paused and twisted her lips. "Things I should have told you a long time ago."

Lizbet, of course, knew that her mother had secrets. The many books she'd read told her that very few lived in isolation the way that she and her mother did. There had to be a world beyond the island, a place peopled with more than friendly postmen and the occasional visitor.

An engine roared. A big beautiful boat slid into the cove. Sunlight sparkled off its shiny chrome and glass. This boat was bigger than anything Lizbet had ever seen.

"How?" Rose whispered, dropping her hoe. "He's found me."

"Who is it, Mama?" Lizbet asked.

Rose quickly bent and retrieved her hoe, but this time she carried it like a weapon. "No questions, love. I need you to run and hide."

"Hide? Where? Why?"

Rose shook her hoe at Lizbet. "I said no questions! Go to the woods. There's the old shack where Daugherty brewed her ale, go there." Rose sucked in a deep breath. "No one can trespass in the woods," she muttered beneath her breath.

Lizbet's memories of Daugherty were vague, but she knew the shack. "But what about you?"

Rose gripped her hoe like a sword. "I'll join you soon. Now go."

Lizbet picked up her shovel for no other reason than her mom had a hoe and ran into the woods. Wordsworth loped beside her.

"Who is he?" Lizbet asked the birds flying above her.

"A big man," a swallow answered.

"A wolf creature," a robin put in.

"Hide in my tree," a squirrel called out as Lizbet ran past. *"It's hollow inside. He'll never find you."*

"Thank you, but no," Lizbet said, her pace slowing. She wasn't sure she wanted to hide from this man and his large boat. A wicked part of her wanted him to find her and take her to the cities where people and buildings resided. She had read of cars, trucks, and helicopters but never seen one. Occasionally, an airplane would fly overhead, so she knew—sort of—what a plane looked like from a great distance. But all other vehicles were nothing more than what her imagination could conjure up. She had a bicycle, a rusted contraption, but had never seen a motorcycle. There was so very much that she'd never seen, and this man, this stranger, may have seen everything. Maybe he could show her—introduce her to this word beyond the island. Her thoughts ticked over places she'd like to visit: London, Paris, Rome, New York, and Sherwood Forest.

"This man is not your friend," Wordsworth warned her.

A friend. Lizbet ached for a friend, but even as she did so, a wave of guilt washed over her because she knew her mother should be enough. Her mother worked hard to keep them safe, to provide food and warmth, to supply the books for Lizbet's entertainment and education. Lizbet knew her mother had sacrificed her own life—a life with John —to keep Lizbet sheltered from the world and its evil men and cunning women.

But what if I don't want to be sheltered? The thought was so astounding it halted her. Lizbet froze on the path to Daugherty's shack.

Wordsworth pressed his nose to the back of her leg, urging her to go on.

I don't want to be here anymore, Lizbet thought.

"Hurry, hurry, hurry," a friendly squirrel chattered.

"No!" Lizbet found her voice.

"Go! Go! Go!" The crows swooped around her.

"No! I don't think so."

"Not safe! Not safe! Not safe!" the crows contended.

Slowly, Lizbet began picking her way toward the shack because she knew and trusted the crows. They were much more clever than most of the animals and were almost never wrong. Although, unlike Wordsworth, they were self-serving.

"Why don't you think it's safe?" Lizbet asked the crows.

"A gun! A gun! A gun!" the birds responded.

"He has a gun?" Lizbet halted again. She'd read about guns. They were mostly used and possessed by villains and soldiers, and as far as she knew, there weren't any wars being waged on the island... which could only mean that this man meant them harm. "I have to warn my mom!"

"Go to Daugherty's shack as your mom asked," Wordsworth said. "I will protect your mom."

Lizbet brushed past him, heading for her mother. Moments later, her knees buckled as a blinding pain slammed onto the top of her head.

Sometime during the short drive from his dad's condo to his mom's house, the gray skies had begun to drizzle. Not quite rain, and yet wet enough to coat the glass with a barely-there mist. The windshield wipers let out a squeak as they scraped back and forth.

As he drove, Declan's dad switched from one talk radio station to another. The political pundits grated on Declan's nerves, and the sports radio stations had only grim predictions. Declan leaned his head against the passenger side window and wished he was already at Duke.

Finally, his dad turned off the radio and cleared his throat. "Does your mom know?"

"I'm going to tell her tonight."

"She won't like it." Which was code for she won't help pay. But Declan wasn't expecting her to, because financial help from her meant strings attached to his stepfather, and those were strings Declan couldn't afford to pull.

"Mr. Neal said he'd give me more hours," Declan said.

His dad sucked in his lower lip and slid him a glance.

"I know it won't cover the tuition," Declan said. "I'll

get a second job during the summer. I'll make it work." Declan's thoughts went to his Grandfather Forsythe, his mom's dad. According to his mom, he was as rich and old as Satan and twice as mean. His mom hadn't spoken to him since she left for college, but Declan knew she occasionally received payouts from her trust fund and supposedly when the old man died, Gloria would be his only beneficiary. But as his mom said, men older and meaner than Satan don't want to die because then they have to face God and be accountable for their sins.

Declan's dad tightened his grip on the steering wheel and the unspoken words *just go to the state university* hung in the air. The University of Washington was, of course a great school. The UW had offered him a scholarship. And he could live at home—which was exactly why Duke was so appealing. Not only would he not be living at home, he'd be living on the other side of the country, away from his stepfather. Away from the parental drama.

His dad flipped on the blinkers, adding a clicking sound to the intermittent screech of the windshield wipers. The car rolled through the gates of Godwin Estates.

"Do you want me to go in with you?"

"No." The last thing Declan wanted was for his dad to measure antlers with his stepfather. In those competitions, his dad always lost.

"You sure?" His dad cleared his throat. "Do you want me to talk to your mom? She has her own money, you know."

He knew. His mom was a successful real estate agent. She often hired him to play the host at open houses for the mansions she listed. She had a theory that if you're going to sell something, you might as well make it something big because it takes just as much effort to sell something big as it takes to selling something small. Gloria Godwin didn't like to play small. She wore big jewelry, had big hair, and toted around a very big portfolio of homes on Queen Anne's Eastside. She also had a big heart, which is probably why she had married Declan's dad, and why she would probably help pay for Declan's tuition if he asked.

But he wasn't going to ask.

Declan hated his stepfather that much. He'd rather work six jobs than be indebted to Gaylord Godwin in anyway.

The Honda pulled up in front of the French chateau monstrosity his mother called home. As if on cue, the drizzle turned to a solid sheet of rain.

Declan pulled his hood over his head, bracing himself.

"Give your mom and Godwin my best," his dad said.

Really? Why did his dad have to be so nice? Declan tried not to, but he despised his dad's good nature. When the car came to a full stop, Declan opened the door and a wet cold breeze blew into the car.

"See you Sunday night," Declan said without looking at his dad.

Godwin's husky, Rufus met him at the door. "Hello?" Declan called, dropping his overnight bag in the entry with a hollow thud.

No one answered.

He made his way to the kitchen, his mom's refuge, while Rufus loped after him, clicking his nails on the travertine tile. On the counter, Declan found a note from his mom propped up beside a plate of homemade peanut butter cookies.

Hope you brought your fancy duds because we're going to celebrate! Marciano's, eight o'clock! Be ready!

Did his mom know about Duke? How could she? He'd just gotten the acceptance that morning. But then, his mom had always had a weird mom-intuition vibe. And she had an amazing network of friends. Had she heard it from one of the teachers or counselors at school?

Declan scratched his head and picked up a cookie.

Rufus sat beside Declan's Converse shoes and gazed up at him, looking much more humble and pathetic than a giant husky ever should.

Declan had compassion and fed him a cookie.

Rufus inhaled it in one bite.

"Don't tell!" Declan commanded the dog.

Rufus licked his lips and shook his paw at Declan, asking for more.

"I don't think so," Declan said.

Rufus nudged Declan with his snout as if trying to tell him something. Declan brushed the dog away.

A buzzing interrupted the doggy-exchange. A slim black phone vibrated on the granite countertop. He knew it had to belong to Godwin as his mom's phone had a faux diamonds encrusted case. Declan glanced at the text message from a Leo Cabriolet. Meet at eight. Usual place.

He briefly wondered who this Leo might be, but then the message registered. Eight. The same time they were supposed to be celebrating at Marciano's. Declan's heart lifted as he realized this might mean that for once he'd have his mother's company without sleazy Godwin.

It might have been Declan's imagination, but it seemed as if Heaven chose that moment to turn off the rain. A faint ray of sun shone through the windows as Declan popped another cookie in his mouth, gathered up his overnight bag, and bounded up the circular staircase to the room where he typically stayed when he visited his mom.

From Declan's Research
"A single sunbeam is enough to drive
away many shadows."
—Francis of Assisi

Chapter Three

A gentle rain bathed Lizbet's face. She blinked open her eyes. Light filtered through the branches. She found the shifting greens surprising, and she tried to process her surroundings. Where was she? Why did her ears ring? Why did her head pound like bongo drums?

She struggled to sit up. For once, the forest remained eerily quiet.

"Where is everyone?" she asked.

No squirrels, no scurrying mice, no lurking fox, no skulking opossum.

Lizbet closed her eyes against the pain and rested on the dirty ground. "Mom? Wordsworth?"

"They're not here, Lizbet," a familiar voice said. *"I'm sorry."*

Lizbet bolted up and for a moment, her vision blurred. Dizziness twirled behind her eyes. She focused on the cat beside her. "What do you mean you're sorry?"

Tennyson looked toward the distant bay. *"He's gone now. You're safe. Follow me."*

Lizbet had never taken instructions from the cat before, but she did so now. Using a nearby tree trunk as a brace, she stood. Her legs quivered as she walked. "What happened to me?"

Tennyson stalked through the forest like a lion hunting prey. *"Norrie dropped a tree branch on your head."*

Lizbet paused. "She what?"

"It was for your own good. You should thank her."

"Thank her? I'm going to kill her. I'm going to turn her into an eagle stew."

Tennyson didn't reply for a long moment. *"You mustn't talk so casually of death as Norrie just postponed your own."*

A chill passed through Lizbet. "What do you mean?"

Tennyson didn't answer.

Lizbet followed without any further questions. She knew as soon as she saw the house that something was terribly wrong. The windows wore a blank empty look as if they were the eyes of the dead. Ignoring her raging pain, Lizbet ran. "Mom!"

Inside, the towers of books had been toppled. Bent bindings, crumpled pages, the books were scattered around the room in disarray. Among the chaos lay Rose curled in the fetal position. Lizbet stumbled forward, knelt at her mother's side and picked up her limp wrist.

A steady pulse thrummed beneath Lizbet's fingers. "She's

alive!" Lizbet called out, but only the cat could hear her. "I have to do something. I have to get help." How many days until Leonard the postman arrived? Lizbet tried to remember the date, and failed.

"I have to do something..." Lizbet stared at the cat. "I have to get help. I don't know what to do." She sucked in a long breath. "Where's Wordsworth?"

The cat gazed back at her with unblinking hazel eyes. *"I'm sorry,"* he said.

Panic welled in Lizbet's throat. She pushed to her feet. "Where's Wordsworth?" she repeated more loudly.

Tennyson's tail twitched to the left.

Lizbet saw what she didn't want to see: her dog lying in a pool of blood.

"He died a hero," Tennyson said.

"No!" Lizbet choked back a sob and stumbled toward him. She fell to her knees and pressed her ear to his furry, silent side. Despite his thick coat, he felt cold. Too still.

"You don't have time to grieve," Tennyson said. *"You need to find help for your mother."*

"And I don't know how to do that," Lizbet sobbed.

"You must find a way."

Panic and pain made Lizbet mean. "That's really easy for you to say because you're a cat. I'm a person. Almost a grown person, and I don't have a clue..."

Wait. She knew one person who would help. John. But she didn't know his last name. She stumbled toward

her mom's office, a place that her mother usually kept under lock and key, but today the door gaped open. Lizbet hurried inside, feeling like she had entered the Forbidden City. Papers littered the desk. Lizbet had always known her mother to be organized, if not tidy, and so she knew that someone other than her mom had to be responsible for the office's chaotic state.

"Tennyson, how long was I passed out?"

The cat didn't answer, but jumped up onto the desk and began licking his left paw, reminding Lizbet that the cat detested being wrong, and so when he didn't know an answer, he simply refused to provide one. She had never known him to hazard a guess.

Lizbet did some mental calculations. It had been morning when the stranger had arrived and now the sun hung on the horizon, giving the stranger ample time to search the office. Had he found what he was looking for? What could he have wanted? Rose led a very simple life.

Tennyson jumped onto a small table beneath a cupboard and pawed the door. *"In here."*

Lizbet found a black box cradling a small device with buttons numbered zero through nine. It immediately it flashed with lighted icons when she picked it up.

Tennyson huffed. *"It's called a phone. It's a device for communication."*

"I know what a phone is," Lizbet said. I just didn't know what one looks like, she thought.

"Obviously," Tennyson said.

Lizbet pushed the small red button. Recalling the dozens of murder mysteries she'd read, she pushed the numbers 911.

"Emergency," a voice responded.

Lizbet was so startled she nearly dropped the phone. Tennyson's steady gaze bolstered her. "I'd like to report a murder," Lizbet said, her voice warbling as she gazed at Wordsworth's inert body.

Marciano's sat on the Chebar River. Declan's mom would rather sit at tables on the deck overlooking the thick canopy of trees than be inside. Beneath the chatter of conversations and the clinking of cutlery, Declan picked up on the sounds of the tumbling river, the buzzing insects, and his mom's French manicured nails tapping impatiently on the table. Her smile grew increasingly brittle as each minute ticked past.

"Your stepfather should be here soon," she said through tight lips.

Declan snagged his third roll from the breadbasket. The waiter, Chaz, had called them garlic knots. His mother called them oily carbs. Declan thought of them as filler food—good for not only eating, but also for something to do while his mom tapped out a frustrated rhythm with her fork while she waited for Godwin to show.

Declan tried to understand what had driven his mom from his dad to someone like Godwin. Godwin was the embodiment of everything his dad was not. Ambitious and driven, Godwin hid his true nature beneath a sheen of charm and a headful of hair gel. Declan found his stepfather has slippery as the garlic knot—and doubly distasteful.

Gloria's phone buzzed with a text. Declan knew from the twist of her lips that the text was from Godwin.

"Your stepfather's run into traffic," she said, flashing an over-bright smile at him. "We may as well order."

Declan glanced at his watch. Eight-thirty six. He thought about telling his mom about the text he'd seen earlier demanding Godwin's presence elsewhere at this same time, but decided against it for the simple reason that he was happy to have his mom to himself for the moment. He loved her with a quiet ache, despite his anger and disappointment that she'd chosen Godwin over his father. In his heart, he knew she didn't belong with either of these men. The one too kind and indolent, the other smarmy. He tried to think of someone who would suit his mom and the only image he could come up with was Clark Kent.

Lizbet sat in the overstuffed chair by the hearth. Despite the fire raging in the grate, she shivered from fear and shock. The man in the black uniform across from her ran his fingers through his pale thin hair. He had introduced himself as Officer Mayer. He looked about her mother's age, but his skin was blotchy, and his waist thick. He held a small black device in his hand. Earlier, he had asked if he could record their conversation. She wasn't quite sure what this meant, so she had complied.

"Let's try this again. You say your mother's name is Rose Wood, and your name is Lizbet Wood." He kept on repeating the same questions as if he expected Lizbet's answers to change.

Lizbet nodded.

He sat back, folded his arms across his chest, and lifted one ankle to rest it on his opposite knee. "And yet, there's no known record of either of you. According to our records, Rose Wood died more than ten years ago."

"Can I see my mother now?"

"Your mother is being airlifted to the Queen Anne General."

"General what?"

Officer Mayer looked blankly at her.

She thought him especially dimwitted, but since she had very little experience with men, she had no one to compare him to. "The word general is an adjective," she informed him, "meaning widespread, or affecting most people. It can also be a military rank."

"I know what general means!" Officer Mayer said.

"Well, which is it?"

"Queen Anne General Hospital," Officer Mayer growled.

"Oh." Comprehension dawned, making her feel like the dimwitted one. "She's going to be okay, though, right?" Lizbet blinked back tears.

A look of compassion swept over Officer Mayer's face. "We can't be sure."

"They'll try and blame you," Tennyson said. He sat perched on the back of Lizbet's chair.

Lizbet twisted and pulled the cat onto her lap. "What? Why do you say that?"

"The staff at Queen Anne General is used to dealing with Jane Does," Officer Mayer said. "They'll take good care of her, even without insurance."

But Lizbet wasn't waiting for his answer.

"They think you did it," Tennyson said. *"The mice heard the officers talking outside. It will be easier for them if they can arrest you. You need to tell them about the man on the boat."*

"H-h-ow?" Lizbet's thoughts stuttered. She tried to rally them. "The man in the boat that came here this morning. He's the one who did this. He bashed in my mother's head and killed my dog." Lizbet's voice faltered. "You have to find him."

Officer Mayer cleared his throat. "We'll do our best. In the meantime, let me fill you in on what's going to happen next. We'll be moving you to Blueberry Fields. It's a home for kids in the foster care system. A case worker will be assigned, and will help organize a search for any family."

An idea struck Lizbet. "I'm eighteen! I'm an adult." Although, according to her mom, she was seventeen.

Suspicion flickered in his eyes.

"I'm small, like my mom."

Their diminutive size was about the only characteristic Lizbet and her mother shared. Rose had fair skin and strawberry blonde hair. Outdoors, she always wore a large floppy straw hat to keep her nose and ears from turning red. She never left the house without sunglasses, claiming that the sun blinded her light blue eyes. Bugs swarmed after Rose, preferring her creamy skin to Lizbet's swarthiness. Lizbet with her green eyes and skin never worried about the sun or mosquitoes.

"We're moon and sun," Rose liked to say. "It is ourselves. Both and one."

"And we don't have any family," Lizbet said.

"You might think that, but it might not necessarily be the case."

"I'm positive there isn't family."

Officer Mayer flipped his notebook closed—a clear signal that he disagreed with her.

"Even if we do have family, don't you think there would be a reason my mom made a significant effort to avoid them?" Her mom had always said that she and Lizbet were all they needed. Lizbet's throat tightened as she realized how wrong her mom had been, because without Rose, Lizbet was completely alone.

"Any ideas on who or what your mom was hiding from?"

"What makes you think she was hiding?"

Officer Mayer waved his hand around at the stone cottage with its closed shutters making Lizbet see it from his point of view. The cottage was almost completely overrun by ivy, making it look like a hill in a field. Even the slate roof had a healthy covering of moss. Lizbet wondered if their home would even be distinguishable from the air, or if it would blend into the wooded countryside.

"We didn't always live alone, you know."

Officer Mayer raised an eyebrow and waited for her to continue.

"Daugherty lived here, too."

"And what happened to her?"

"She died years ago." Lizbet barely remembered Daugherty, but the intense feeling of sadness she'd felt so long ago returned and touched her for just a moment.

"Was there a proper funeral? Was it reported? Did you get a death certificate?"

"I was just a child. I don't remember anything, really. She made and sold blackberry wine. I can show you her shack if you'd like."

Officer Mayer twisted his lips and looked unhappy.

A red-breasted robin flew to the window and pecked at the screen. *"Footprints in the cove. Footprints in the cove."*

Lizbet sat up. "I want to show you the footprints in the cove. A man's footprints—you'll want to see them right? So you can know if you're looking for a big-footed murderer?"

"This is not yet a murder investigation."

"The man killed my dog and nearly my mom!"

Officer Mayer dipped his head, acknowledging his mistake.

Fragments of an old murder mystery involving a child witness came back to her. Lizbet climbed to her feet, scooped up the cat, and headed for her mom's office.

"Now see here, where you going?" Officer Mayer demanded.

"I'm getting my mom's camera. I'm going to take pictures of the footprints in the cove and then I'm going to compare them to the shoes of all your men who, for all I know, have been mucking up a crime scene." Lizbet paused in the doorway of her mom's office. "You can't just haul me off to who-knows-where, and I'm pretty sure you shouldn't even be talking to me without a lawyer present. We're done."

Righteous indignation carried Lizbet down to the cove, but once she got away from Officer Mayer and his posse of beer-bellied men, tears crowded behind her eyes. The enormity of her situation settled on her shoulders and weighed her down. She didn't even know how or where her mom developed their film, let alone a million and one other things her mom did to make their isolated life on the island possible. What would she do now? Without her mom, the long winter nights and drizzly gray days would be unbearable.

"You still have me," Tennyson said as he trotted through the long grass beside her.

Lizbet gave the cat a bleak smile, because, as always, Tennyson was as intuitive as a crystal ball. And right now, Lizbet needed a crystal ball.

"And us," a crow called.

"You guys are always good for a bump on the head," Lizbet muttered, worry turning her mood sour.

"We saved your life," Tennyson said.

Lizbet sniffed as she stalked through the field and down the bank that led to the cove. The police boat was tied to the dock and bumped against the wood pilings with the falling and rising waves. The grass where the gigantic helicopter had landed was smashed and twisted about. Much like her insides.

She closed her eyes against the memories of her inert mom being carried away on a stretcher and lifted into the noisy grasshopper-like machine. Blood had covered her mom's face and stained her pale hair. Her eyes had remained mercifully closed. Her hand had dangled from the stretcher like a silent plea for Lizbet to follow.

Lizbet still couldn't understand why she'd been left behind.

"Footprints?" Lizbet asked the bird.

The robin swooped down and settled on a patch of smashed grass. Sure enough, footprints, but unless she was able to compare them to the police officers' boots, there wouldn't be any way to know if they belonged to them or someone else. She snapped a few pictures and followed the footsteps to the beach. In the sand, one print clearly showed an emblem. Knowing it would be gone as soon as the tide came in, Lizbet took a picture.

"The men! The men! The men!" the gulls cried.

Lizbet looked up to see Officer Mayer and his band of men approaching. She waved them over. "This is very distinctive."

"Wellingtons," the youngest officer said. He had chocolate-colored hair and eyes, and unlike his portly peers, a swimmer's build. "Pretty expensive boots."

Officer Mayer scratched his chin. "Looks like a size fourteen."

"A big guy," another officer said.

The officer with the chocolate eyes smiled at Lizbet. "I'm guessing that you nor your mom wear a size fourteen."

Officer Mayer nodded at an officer. "Let's take some pictures." His voice sounded heavy and drained, as if the thought of doing any actual investigative police work made him tired.

Later, when the sun had sunk into the Sound and Lizbet was alone with her thoughts, she padded into her mom's office. This was forbidden territory, but since her mom wasn't here to stop her, or to answer questions, or to share their evening meal, Lizbet sat at the desk. It felt wrong. But then, everything was wrong. Her mom made everything right. Lizbet couldn't imagine a life without her. The

thought that her mom could disappear, like Daugherty, made Lizbet's breath catch in her throat.

She clenched her hands and tried to envision a life off of the island. All her mom's grim tales flooded her thoughts. Lewd men. Conniving women. Greed. Lust. Coldhearted liars. Lizbet pressed both of her palms to her eyes, trying to shut out the images her mom had painted for so long.

Not everyone could be bad, could they? Leonard the postman seemed like an okay guy. The police officers had seemed lazy, but not malicious.

But Lizbet knew one thing for sure, she would rather take her chances in a world full of people, good and bad, then live alone on the island. For not the first time, she wondered how her mom paid for the utilities—the electricity and water. And did her mom own their house outright? Or was there a mortgage? And why did Officer Mayer say there wasn't a record of her mom? Could it be that Rose Wood wasn't her mom's real name? So, why had she changed it?

Curiosity mingled with anger and frustration made Lizbet rifle through the desk drawers. She wanted to find answers, but instead she found paperclips, staples, receipts, and a collection of drawings by Lizbet's younger self.

Lizbet sat back and spun in her chair. Her eye caught sight of one of the bookshelves that held an assortment of Rose's agricultural books: Composting 101, Living Off the Land and Loving It, Dirt Farming for Dummies. For all she knew, neither she nor her mom had looked at those

books in years, and yet they were dust free. The shelves above and below had books as equally as mind-numbingly dull and they all had a light layer of dust on them—as all boring books should. But one particular shelf wasn't dusty at all.

Lizbet sprung from the chair, pulled the dust-free books to the floor, and discovered a hidden safe secured with a thick padlock. She stared at it for a few moments before she started to work at it. The spinning dial clicked, but little else.

She rested her butt on the desk and drummed her fingers on her thighs, thinking. Something she read in a Sherlock Holmes's novel came back to her. She quickly jotted down the alphabet and assigned each letter a number, A being one. Eighteen for R, fifteen for O, nineteen for S, five for E. Nothing. Then she did the same thing for Lizbet and the lock fell open.

Lizbet pulled open the door and discovered a collection of papers.

Answers.

From Declan's Research
"Ignorance more frequently begets confidence than does
knowledge: it is those who know little, and not those who
know much, who so positively assert that this or that
problem will never be solved by science."
—Charles Darwin

Chapter Four

Declan sat halfway in on the third pew from the front, on the left. According to Godwin, his family had been occupying this pew for more than three decades. Declan liked it because of the way the sunlight filtered through the stain-glass window of Christ with a flock of sheep. Also, it was not too close to the pastor, who, when excited, tended to spit as he preached. Since the pastor had been excited every time Declan had attended services with his mom and stepfather, Declan appreciated the fact that Godwin's predecessors had chosen not to sit in the splash zone.

But there was a boatload of things he didn't appreciate. Number one, and this was a biggie, it was a pew—in a church. Number two, Nicole Gunner and Jason Norbit sat two rows ahead of him on the right. He liked Nicole almost as much as he disliked Jason.

While Declan's mom, Godwin, and about a third of the rest of the congregation picked up their hymnals and followed the direction of the music chorister, Declan folded his arms, leaned back against the pew, and skated a glance at his mom. Until her marriage to Godwin, he wouldn't have thought she possessed a religious bone. When she'd lived with him and his dad, they'd never practiced or embraced any religion. Their only nods at spirituality had been a Christmas tree and an Easter basket. But now, his mom sang praises to a God that Declan didn't know and couldn't understand. Didn't want to know or understand.

He glanced around the room, recognizing some of Eastside's power players—the mayor, the president of the school board, the CEO of Allied Digital. She wouldn't align herself to a faith for business contacts, would she? The thought was so awful, he immediately dismissed it and replaced it with memories of his mom pushing him on the swings, taking him on the merry-go-round, and reading him *Goodnight Moon*.

He leaned forward and put his head in his hands, but not before he caught sight of Jason draping his arm around Nicole's shoulders and pulling her close. Declan ran his finger beneath his collar and prayed to the God he didn't believe in that he could be anywhere else but here. If this God was so all-powerful it wouldn't be such a big deal to transport Declan to a McDonalds or a sports park.

As expected, his prayer went unanswered.

Lizbet's world tipped more and more off balance with each new piece of information. From the receipts and invoices, it seemed that her mom had once owned and operated a successful blackberry wine business with a variety of distributors up and down the west coast.

A fat manila envelope sat in the back of the safe. She pulled it out and found hundreds of hundred-dollar bills stuffed inside. She wouldn't need all of it, would she? Would it be safer to leave it in the safe, or take it with her? How much did things cost in Queen Anne? She'd need a place to stay, something to eat... what else? What about the medical costs? She took it all out.

Lizbet sucked in a deep breath, selected a few of the most telling papers, and went to her mom's room. She towed a dusty suitcase out from underneath her mom's bed and went to fill it. She had a collection of lightweight cotton skirts, sandals, sweaters, as well as Levi overalls. She wondered how people on the mainland dressed. In some of the books, clothes were described in great detail, but most of those were historical novels. She knew she couldn't show up looking like Scarlett O'Hara in a hoop skirt. How sad that her only contemporary fashion indicator was Leonard the postman. She hoped that not everyone in Queen Anne wore knee-length shorts and a blue shirt with their names stamped over their breast pockets.

But how she looked didn't matter. She needed to find her mom and make sure she was being taken care of. And then she needed to find the man with the size-fourteen shoes and make him pay for what he did to her mom, her dog, and her turned-up-side-down world.

"She wouldn't even make you a loan?" Disbelief tinged Declan's dad's tone.

"It's okay, I wouldn't have taken it anyway." Declan tightened his grip on his overnight bag while his dad's foot grew increasingly heavy on the gas pedal. Speed and recklessness through the Queen Anne traffic was the only sign of the anger Declan knew had to be boiling just beneath his dad's affable face.

His dad white-knuckled the steering wheel. "I can't believe..."

"Forget it. I don't want to owe Godwin anything."

"But—" his dad sputtered.

"Mom said they're both up to their eyeballs in that housing development."

"What housing development?"

Declan knew his dad would no sooner invest in a housing development than take a trip to the moon. "That one." At that moment, they happened to pass a giant billboard with a picture of a two-story house with a stone

façade complete with a turret. The caption read, *Dreams really can come true! Live out yours on Royalty Ridge.*

His dad's normally tanned skin won from his hours spent at the golf course, tennis court, and on his bike turned a shade pink. "She wasn't always like this, you know," he said.

"I know."

"She was cute. Bouncy. We were just kids."

Declan, of course knew the story. It was a classic teen romance. The high school quarterback marrying the head cheerleader. They had made it last longer than it probably should have. "It's okay. Really. I got a job walking Mrs. Reilly's dog."

"In addition to everything else..."

"I know it's a lot, but it'll be worth it. Principal Martin said he'd put my name on the tutor list."

His dad elbowed him. "Why are you such a brainiac?"

Declan grinned. "'Cuz I'm your kid."

Declan's grandmother called his dad a full package of beauty, brains, and brawn. His Aunt Gertie, his mom's sister, called him a thoroughbred racehorse that never left the starting gate. They were both right. And despite, or maybe because of, the beauty, brains, brawn, and divorce, his dad, Declan knew, was basically just what he'd always been: a happy pony. He liked teaching math and coaching football for East End High and playing golf, tennis, soccer, and baseball in the summer, and skiing, snow-shoeing,

and ice-fishing in the winter. He didn't want to be up to his eyeballs, or even his toes, in real estate deals. Or deals of any kind.

And Declan didn't want to deal with Godwin. He saw it as dealing with the devil.

When Leonard came the next day, Lizbet was sitting on a big rock in the cove waiting for him. She explained what had happened while he stared at her through his thick glasses. Several emotions flashed across his face while she told her story, but the one that lingered was compassion.

"I'll get you to Queen Anne General Hospital," he said. "But I know for dead certain that they won't be letting you bring that creature inside." He pointed at Tennyson curled in a basket on Lizbet's lap.

Lizbet gazed down at the orange tabby and panic stuttered her thoughts. Going to Queen Anne would be hard, but going without Tennyson would be impossible.

"We'll cross that bridge when we get to it," Tennyson told her with a flick of his tail.

Lizbet lifted her chin. "I'll leave him with... friends while I visit my mom."

Leonard's expression told her he suspected she didn't have any friends. "So, you got you a place to stay? You're not going to try sleeping under a bridge, or anything,

right? Cuz I can't have that on my conscience. Queen Anne's a big city and could swallow whole a little gal like you without a hiccough."

Lizbet tightened her lips. She didn't need Leonard to make her any more scared than she already was. "I appreciate your concern. I really do. But I'd appreciate you even more if we could just leave already."

Leonard chuckled. "Well, don't get your panties in bunch. It'll take us a good long time to complete my route. Probably won't be getting back to Queen Anne until dinner time."

"That's fine." Lizbet rummaged through the macramé bag she had hung around her shoulder and pulled out a bottle.

"What's this?" Leonard asked.

"It's my mom's blackberry wine—as a thank you."

Leonard smacked his lips. "Well, now, that's a mighty fine thank you."

"I'm glad you think so," Lizbet said, right before she climbed onto his boat and settled down on a cushioned bench beneath the bimini top. She placed Tennyson's basket beside her, smoothed down her skirt, and pulled a P.D. James murder mystery out of her bag. She typically preferred cozy mysteries to police procedurals, but right now she needed all the instruction on crime solving she could get, even if it happened to be British, and she didn't know where else to find it.

And what did it mean to get your panties in a bunch? Did panties come in bunches? She and her mom got theirs

in packages. Leonard delivered them, so he probably knew more about where her panties came from than she did. This thought so unsettled her that she stewed about it for a long time. Everything she owned had come from her mom. But how had her mom gotten her panties as well as everything else? They grew most of their own food—canning and storing their fruits and vegetables for the long winter months. But some things—oatmeal, whole wheat flour, toiletries, books—were delivered by Leonard. Her mom must have bought and paid for them, but how? Had the blackberry wine business been that successful? And if so, why had her mom walked away from it?

Lizbet let the questions bubble inside her until she thought she'd explode. When she decided she couldn't take anymore, she did what she always did when stressed. She drew her bookmark out and lost herself between the pages of her novel.

A light rain fell and a heavy cloud hovered over the Queen Anne skyline. To Lizbet, the gray-shrouded city looked like it had escaped the pages of a science fiction novel. She clutched Tennyson's basket and worried she'd made a mistake. Raindrops collected on the windshield and Leonard's plastic poncho, but he didn't seem to mind. Lizbet, sitting a row behind him was drier and probably warmer, but her mood matched the drizzly weather.

"We should go home," she whispered. "I don't belong here."

"Not yet," the cat replied. *"But you will."* He let out a long meow. *"The mice will be so hard to find among all this concrete."*

"I won't let you starve," she told the cat. "Maybe we can purchase mice... somehow."

Leonard chuckled and shot her a quick glance over his shoulder. "You know you can buy canned cat food, right?"

"They put mice in cans?" Lizbet asked. Why that seemed so much crueler than letting Tennyson stalk and eat mice, she didn't know, but it did. At least with stalking and pouncing the mice had a sporting chance. Locking the poor things up in cans seemed wrong in so many ways.

Leonard let out a belly laugh and his potato-shaped middle jiggled. "No, silly. I'm not exactly sure what they put in those little cans. It smells like the devil's butt, but the cats love it. Well, except for the Siamese. There's no pleasing those guys. I should know, I got myself one of those finicky creatures."

Tennyson looked as skeptical as Lizbet felt. She ran her fingers through the cat's fur while Leonard guided his little postal boat into the busy harbor. Several others manning their own watercrafts called out to them and Leonard waved at all of them. These men and women watched Lizbet with questioning eyes, but Lizbet had so many questions of her own, she ignored their stares.

Buildings as tall as trees. Air as rank as the slough. The sounds melded together, completely indistinguishable one from another. Gulls wheeled over her head, but she

couldn't catch their words. They were hungry, worried, and scared. Lizbet tightened her grip on Tennyson's basket.

"Let me take care of a few things at the postal center," Leonard said. "It'll take me awhile, but if you don't mind sitting tight in my car, I can drop you off at Queen Anne General on my way home. Or, if you'd rather, you can walk. It's just five blocks that way."

Five blocks? What composed a block?

Leonard must have read the panic in her eyes, because he pointed out the large gray building on the hill. "It's that place right there. Although, like I said, you won't be able to take the cat inside."

Lizbet nodded, thanked Leonard, ignored his friends, and headed toward the hospital. She didn't want to sit and wait. She needed to be up and doing something. If she kept busy, maybe her mind would stop running in circles. Juggling her suitcase, the macramé bag, and Tennyson's basket, she left the marina and pier. Tennyson remained uncharacteristically quiet. Lizbet guessed he was as cowed as she was by the noise, sights, and smells of the city.

As they moved further from the wharf, the air turned less briny but heavier with exhaust from the machines roaring through the streets. She found herself thinking, this must be a car, this must be a bus, but what is the contraption that travels through the air on the suspended track? What is the tall tower looking like a turtle stuck on a fence post?

Like the buildings and vehicles, the people also came in all shapes, sizes, and colors. She immediately knew she hadn't needed to worry about what to wear. Only a very few wore uniforms as strict as Leonard's. Bearded men in shorts and flip-flops. Women in long skirts. Girls in pants so tight they looked like they were wearing stockings all the way up their legs. Men in blazers with crisp white shirts and colorful ties. A man in a white lab coat that flapped as he walked. A mother in jeans and a sweater pushing a baby stroller. A fat, curly haired, pink-cheeked baby waved his bottle at Lizbet. She smiled back.

And there was an African American. She had never seen one before in real life. His hair, fashioned into a multitude of tiny braids, was nothing like the African America female she spotted across the street. And there was a redheaded man in a kilt. She wondered if he truly didn't wear underwear beneath his skirt, but decided asking this would be as rude as asking if she could touch the black man's hair. Although, she really wanted to touch the black curly hair and peek beneath the redheaded man's kilt.

The sensory overload tempted Lizbet to sit on a street bench and watch the tide of humanity wash past, but the need to find her mother pushed her forward. She kept her eyes on the tall gray building, knowing she'd be disoriented in minutes if she lost sight of it.

She stepped off a curb and several things happened all at once. A bus driver blasted his horn. A car screeched so close that she felt the heat of its engine on her skin. She dropped Tennyson's basket as a hand grabbed her arm and pulled her back onto the sidewalk.

"What are you doing?" A man in a suit held her captive. His bald head glistened from the fine mist falling around them.

She shook away from him. "I'm going to the hospital."

He snorted. "You're going to need the hospital if you step out into traffic like that again."

Traffic. Lizbet glanced at the poles lining the sidewalks. A small box with an illuminated red hand flashed at her. A trio of lights hovered over the street. The cars rushed past, but when the light changed from green to red, the cars pulled to a stop at the painted white lines on the street.

Fascinating. The lights controlled the cars. But how?

"Are you okay?" the man asked.

"No, I'm...Tennyson!" Where was he? His empty basket lay at her feet.

"You're Tennyson?"

"My cat!" She glanced at the street. The cars idled beside her, but she guessed that as soon as the light turned red they would all zoom away and if Tennyson were hiding beneath any of the tires... "Tennyson!"

From Declan's Research
"It is not the strongest of the species that survive,
nor the most intelligent, but the one most
responsive to change."
—Charles Darwin

Chapter Five

Declan pulled his Ford F150 up to the curb in front of Patty's Poodle Palace and slammed his truck into park. The front window had dancing poodle silhouettes painted on it, a pink and white striped awning over the door, and pots filled with pink geraniums on the sill. Just looking at it threatened his manhood. He wondered if Beetle had an opinion on his barbershop... or beauty parlor.

He ducked inside, retrieved the freshly bathed dog, and headed outside as fast as he could. Immediately, a small dark-haired girl standing on the opposite corner caught his attention. She wore a boho skirt, clunky lace-up boots, and a long knotty green sweater, and carried a basket with something orange and furry inside it. Her long dark hair reminded him of someone or something... maybe a raven's wing.

He stopped short when he spotted Nicole on the corner of David and Third.

She raised her hand in a small wave. Nothing like the girl in the boho skirt, Nicole did everything in an understated way. He supposed that was one of the things he liked about her. Her clothes bordered on boring. She wore her hair long, straight, sometimes pulled back, but usually not. Minimal makeup. It was as if she knew she was interesting all on her own and she didn't need to be tarted up.

Of course he wasn't the only one who found her interesting. His dark thoughts turned to Jason Norbit. He almost forgot to wave in return.

Nicole hurried over to him. "Hey, sailor!"

"Hi Nicole." He scrambled for something witty to say. Wanting to compliment her somehow, he searched her face, her clothes, her hair... but found nothing in anyway remarkable. He had to remind himself that this was precisely what he liked about her.

"Who's your friend?" she asked, smiling at him.

Friend? He had friends, of course some were friendlier than others... She knew most of his friends. She'd been in his kindergarten class, so they'd known each other—and their friends—for a long time. Was this a trick question? Had she guessed how he felt about Jason?

She squatted beside him to pet Beetle, and comprehension dawned on Declan like a stack of books hitting him in the head so hard he felt stupid.

"Huh, this is Beetle."

"Beetle, you're a looker!" she crooned at the dog.

"And he smells better than usual, too." What a stupid thing to say. Why would she care how the dog smelled?

Nicole glanced up at him with her large green eyes. "Beagles are known for their sense of smell, right?"

"That's not what I meant..." He jerked his shoulder in the direction of Patty's Poodle Palace. "He just had a bath."

"He's cute. Is he yours?"

"No, I'm..." He thought of Jason's Mercedes and the Norbits' house on Lake Oleander and didn't want to admit he was a paid dog-walker. Not that he was ashamed of having to work. That wasn't it. He just knew some girls cared about money and status. He hoped Nicole wasn't one of those girls. "He belongs to a friend."

Nicole gave Beetle another rub between his ears before she climbed to her feet. "You want to come by tomorrow night? I'm having a party."

Words caught in Declan's throat and for a second he worried they would choke him. "That would be great!" he managed to get out, hoping he didn't sound as eager as he felt.

"Great!" She repeated his word. "I'll see you then." She wiggled her fingers at him, or maybe at Beetle, and turned to go.

He stood on the corner, watching her hair flounce around her shoulders, liking the way the sun glinted on her honey blond curls, and the bounce in her step. After she disappeared into a party supply store, he shook himself, turned and... where was Beetle?

A beagle raced past Lizbet, braying like a wounded donkey as he brushed against her. A flash of orange fur streaked through the crowd.

"Tennyson!" Lizbet took off after the cat. She caught up to the beagle first. Stepping in front of him, she confronted the dog. "What do you think you're doing?" She slapped his nose.

"Cat! Cat! Cat!" The dog brayed and tried to go around her, but Lizbet captured his collar and gave it a sharp tug.

"Listen here, Neanderthal."

"Cat! Cat! Cat!" The dog continued his howl.

Lizbet squatted to eye level and placed her hands on either side of the beagle's head. "You are not going to chase that cat."

The dog met her gaze and dropped to its haunches.

"How did you do that?"

Lizbet looked up into the bluest eyes she'd ever seen. A young man about her age stood in front of her, an empty leash dangling from his hand. His thick hair curled over his forehead.

"He's listening to you. Beetle doesn't listen to anyone unless they're holding raw meat."

"Is that true, Beetle?" Lizbet asked, searching the dog's brown eyes.

"I'm hungry," Beetle whined.

"He says he's hungry." Lizbet relinquished her hold on the dog's collar as the young man took possession of it. For a half-second, his hand brushed hers, sending tingles shooting up her arm.

Lizbet stood and wiped her hands on her skirt.

"He told you that?" The young man smirked as he repositioned the dog's collar and tightened the leash.

"Well, it's pretty obvious. Look at him. He looks like he could use a good meal."

"The cat not only sleeps in my bed, she also eats all my food," Beetle whined.

"Do you have a cat?" Lizbet asked.

"Well, yeah, my mom does but..."

"The cat is probably eating Beetle's food. No wonder he hates cats." Lizbet glanced around. "Now, if you'll excuse me, I have to find mine. Tennyson!"

"Meow."

Tennyson perched on a windowsill ten feet off the ground.

"How did you get up there?"

"Not sure," Tennyson replied. *"Better question, how will I get down?"*

"It's like he's talking to you," the young man said.

"What? No..." Lizbet placed her hands on her hips and gazed up at the cat. "Jump down."

"Not with that creature there."

Lizbet glanced at Beetle. "Can you go away?"

Beetle glared at her, didn't answer, and sat back on his bony haunches.

"It's a public street corner." The young man's lips twitched.

"I know, and you and your dog have every right to be here, but I'm afraid my cat won't come down as long as you're here." He was perhaps the most handsome thing she'd ever seen, and that's what made it so hard to say what had to be said. "Could you please just leave?" She made little shooing motions with her hands.

He balled his fists and placed them on his hips. "What makes you think your cat will come down if I go?"

"Frankly, I don't care if you stay or go, but Beetle must leave, or my cat won't come down."

He planted his feet about hip-distance apart, folded his arms across his chest, and gave Lizbet a defiant what are you going to do about it stare.

Lizbet stared back for several seconds before an idea came to her. She put down her bags, reached for a window ledge about three feet high and swung herself up. A startled woman at a desk on the other side of the window gave her a wide-eyed look. Lizbet, knowing that now, unlike the Scotsman in his kilt, everyone would be able to see her underwear, found another handhold and began to scale the wall.

"What's the problem here?" A man in a police uniform stepped up to them. "Miss, I insist you come down!"

Lizbet looked over her shoulder. "Why?"

He frowned up at her. "It's forbidden... You can't climb the buildings."

"Obviously, I can."

The policeman shook his head.

"Oh, you mean, I shouldn't. Well, why not?"

"You'll get hurt, or you'll hurt someone else." The policeman frowned at her and tapped his foot.

"Seems unlikely," Lizbet called back down. She was now halfway to Tennyson and she wasn't going to come down without the cat. "How can I hurt anyone? Other than Tennyson, I'm the only one up here."

"Get down right now, or I'll have to write you up!" The officer pointed at the sidewalk.

"Am I breaking a law? I don't see any no climbing signs."

"We can't have signs for every little thing!" He stood directly below her.

"You didn't answer my question. Is there a city ordinance against climbing the buildings?"

"Yes!"

Lizbet suspected the officer was lying.

"Go ahead and climb down," Tennyson said. *"You won't do anyone any good if you're in jail."*

She gazed at her cat for half a second before jumping down. Her skirt floated around her before settling back around her knees. It took her a moment to catch her breath and find stability. She pointed a finger at the young man. "His dog chased my cat."

The police officer turned his frown on the young man. "There are leash laws here, son."

The young man blew out a frustrated breath. "He got away from me."

The police officer's lips twitched.

The young man raked his fingers through his thick brown curls. "I know he looks old and slow, but—"

The police officer clapped his hand on the young man's back. "Gotta keep a grip."

Lizbet silently conferred with Tennyson and he meowed back that Lizbet should go to the hospital. He would wait for her on the ledge. While the police officer and the young man talked about leashes and proper pet etiquette, Lizbet slipped away.

It wasn't easy to run with her macramé bag, cat basket, and suitcase banging against her legs as she weaved through the people thronging the busy sidewalk, but she managed to reach the wide double doors of Queen Anne General without knocking anyone over.

She paused on the black rubber mat in front of the entrance. To her amazement, the glass doors slid open. She dropped her bags in surprise.

"Here, let me help you." A man in a dark wool suit that perfectly matched his ebony hair reached for her suitcase.

Lizbet fell to her knees and quickly scooped up the few things that had escaped her bag—a hair brush, a container of lip balm, and her novel.

"You're a James fan?"

His eyes were almost as dark as her own. His thick black hair was brushed away from his face, exposing a widow's peak. A flicker of recognition tingled in the back of her mind. She had met this man before, she was sure of it, but she couldn't say where, how, or when. Looking in his face was like looking at a photograph of a not too distant memory. He was tall, but solid—nothing like the lithe young man who belonged to Beetle—and he had huge hands with strong fingers and blunt nails. An unexpected shiver crawled down her back.

She grabbed her suitcase and novel away from him, said thank you a beat or two later than she should have to be polite, and brushed past him on her way to the large desk with the word INFORMATION hanging above it.

"Can I help you?" a gum-smacking woman asked.

Lizbet cast one more look over her shoulder. The dark man with the widow's peak had left. Tension eased from her shoulders, and she smiled at the middle-aged woman sitting behind the desk.

"I'm looking for Rose Wood," Lizbet said. "Can you tell me what room she's in?"

The woman clicked her fingers on a keyboard and stared at a screen in front of her. "I'm not seeing any Rose Wood," she said after a few smacks of gum. "You could try the Veteran's or the Presbyterian."

Lizbet scratched her head and blinked back a few tears, wondering. Did this woman really think she could ask just

any veteran or Presbyterian about her mom? "Do you know where would I find veterans and Presbyterians?"

"Well, the Presbyterian is about four miles that way, and the Veteran's is near Lake Union."

A heaviness that had nothing to do with the weight of her suitcase and bag pressed down Lizbet's shoulders. "Are you sure?"

Smack, smack. "Absolutely."

Lizbet recalled her conversation with Officer Mayer. He had called her mom a Jane Doe. "Do you, by any chance, have any Jane Does?"

The woman stopped her gum chewing for a moment to give Lizbet a brief are-you-crazy sort of look.

Lizbet mentally shrugged, hugged her bags against herself, and went back out the wide doors. Once again, the magic doors slid open for her, but this time, instead of welcoming her in, she felt as if they were spitting her out.

Not knowing what else to do or where to go, Lizbet spotted a small park on the corner of Horacio and Mabel and she headed toward it. She selected a bench beneath a maple tree and sat down. Now what?

She drummed her fingers on her leg. "Tennyson?"

The cat didn't answer, which made sense. After all, she'd told him to wait for her on the corner of Mabel and Cedar. But she wished he was here now.

A long black car pulled up to the intersection. The windows were darkly tinted, but for a flash of a second,

Lizbet thought she could see the man with the widow's peak sitting in the back seat.

Strange. She knew him somehow. Her thoughts went back to her mom's ginger root. She missed her mom, she worried about her, but at that moment, she was also incredibly angry.

The world couldn't be the hostile, villainous place her mother had made it out to be. Lizbet glanced around the park and saw mothers and babies, children laughing and playing on a swing set, youths riding boards, a young man strumming a guitar, and a girl about her own age sitting on a blanket and reading a book. Not one of them looked as if they possessed an evil bone. Why had her mother kept her locked away from all of this? And how many doses of ginger root had she been given to cloud her memory? For all she knew, her mom may have been going on frequent trips to the city and giving her ginger root tea to make her forget her absence.

Lizbet's whole life seemed like a lie. She didn't know what to believe anymore.

"There you are," a familiar voice said. Tennyson jumped onto her lap.

"How did you find me?"

"I heard you call. We felines have excellent hearing, you know. Let the dogs have their smell—that's a double entendre in case you hadn't picked up on it. Hearing is much more useful and much less distracting than intense olfactory function."

"I suppose," Lizbet muttered, stroking the cat's fur.

"Did you find your mother?"

"There's no one by the name of Rose Wood in the hospital."

"That doesn't mean she's not there."

Lizbet sat up straighter. She glanced at the gigantic building with its myriad of windows and slunk back down feeling defeated. It was so huge. Her mom was just one person. And a small one at that.

"What if I don't find her?" Lizbet asked. What if she died? Lizbet didn't know much about life in the city, but she did know she was incredibly ill-equipped to get along on her own. How long would her money last? And how would she manage when it, too, was gone?

"Who are you looking for?"

Lizbet's head whipped around. The young man and Beetle stood in front of her.

Tennyson rose with a hiss. *"I'll go and see what I can find."*

"There he goes again," the young man said with a grin as he watched the cat bolt across the lawn. "Will you chase him up another wall?"

Lizbet gave him a halfhearted shrug.

"What's your name?"

"Until a few moments ago I thought my name was Lizbet Woods, but now I'm not so sure."

"What changed?" He settled down on the bench beside her and Beetle nestled at his feet.

Lizbet felt his warmth and was drawn to it. She fought the ridiculous desire to tuck her fingers into the pockets of his jacket. She debated on whether or not to confide in him. As he gazed at her with his liquid blue eyes, her hesitation melted and all the warnings that her mother had instilled in her for years and years flitted away on the breeze. So she launched into her story. She told him about the island and her solitary life with her mother leaving out the crucial details of her ability to speak with the animals, because even she, with her lack of social skills, understood that talking to animals just wasn't done. Although, she wasn't sure why not.

When she got to the part about the man in the boat and how her mother had sent her away and when she'd returned she'd found her mother struggling for life, the beautiful boy beside her fell still and she felt his indecision. She read the disbelief in his eyes. "Here I've told you all about me, and I don't even know your name."

He nudged her with his knee. "My name is Declan Lamb."

"Well, Declan Lamb, do you know any veterans or Presbyterians?"

"What? Why?"

She nodded toward the hospital. "The woman told me to check with veterans and Presbyterians if they knew where my mother is, and that just seems so..." she waved her hand in the air as if searching for something to grab, "...random."

He laughed. "You're kidding, right?"

"No."

"Seriously?"

Her eyes welled with tears.

"Oh, geez, I'm sorry. I didn't mean... I'm an ass. Of course you're serious." Although, his expression told her he didn't quite believe her. "I'm sure she meant the veterans' and Presbyterian hospitals."

"Oh." Relief swept through her, although she wasn't quite sure why. She would still have a hard time finding or getting to either place. But finding a hospital seemed much easier than finding a veteran or Presbyterian who might know anything about her mom.

"Meow!" Tennyson sat high in the branches of a maple tree directly above them. Beetle glanced up and shook his tail at the cat, letting his air of bored disinterest slip for a moment.

"I found your mother," Tennyson said. *"They are calling her Daugherty Westmoor."*

Lizbet bounced up.

Declan looked at her as if she'd sprouted cauliflower from her ears.

"I have to go," she told him as she gathered up her bags and hurried back across the street and through the wide magical glass doors that slid open just as she needed them to.

From Declan's Research
"To kill an error is as good a service as,
and sometimes even better than, the
establishing of a new truth or fact."
—Charles Darwin

Chapter Six

She found her mother on the second floor in the ICU unit. Lizbet smiled gratefully at the large pine tree right outside the window, knowing it had played a key role in helping Tennyson find her mother. She dropped her bags and sagged in relief when she saw her mom lying in the hospital bed. Yes, her face was pale, her lips gray, her hair greasy, and she had tubes and wires hooked up to her, but she was still Lizbet's mother—the only person that Lizbet really knew.

Or did she?

Why were they calling her Daugherty Westmoor? Had her mom had been lying to her about her name? And if so, what else had she lied about? And why?

Lizbet brushed aside these dark thoughts. There was

one thing she knew for sure: Her mother loved her. And if she'd lied, she must have had a very good reason. Lizbet pulled a stiff plastic chair away from the wall and dragged it closer to her mom's bedside, so she could sit while holding her mom's hand. Her mom's skin felt cold—nothing like Declan's radiating warmth. "I really need you to wake up now," she said.

Her mom didn't respond.

A tiny nurse in thick white shoes strode into the room. She had a clipboard in her hand, a tag with the name Stacy over her left breast, and a tight smile on her lips.

"Any idea when she'll regain consciousness?" Lizbet asked.

Compassion flickered in the tiny nurse's gaze. "I'm sorry, no. I wish I had a better answer for you."

"Can she hear me?"

"Maybe. There are instances of people who have woken up from a coma with memories of their time asleep."

"What's wrong with her?"

"She's had a head injury. Most coma patients are completely unarousable and unresponsive to even their own needs." Stacy shrugged. "It's hard to say how long this stage will last. It can be for weeks or months. There's no way of knowing when or how she'll wake." Stacy cocked her head. "Are you close?"

"She's my mom."

"Really?"

"Why does that surprise you?"

"You look nothing alike."

Lizbet smiled. "She used to call us salt and pepper."

"What nationality was your father?"

"I never knew my dad."

"Oh, I'm sorry." She blushed. "Please forgive me. I need to learn to mind my own business, but sometimes, as a nurse, it's really hard since nosey questions are a part of my job. After asking people when they last moved their bowels, asking about their fathers seems not as personal."

Lizbet smiled. "It's okay. I'm curious about my dad, too."

"Wouldn't your mom know?"

"You're a nurse. You should get that she might not." Lizbet squeezed her mom's hand. "I still love her."

"There might be more to that story," Stacy said.

"And only she can tell it."

"No, remember, there's someone else, too. But like you said, he didn't stick around to see the ending."

Footsteps pounded down in the hall and soon a small crowd entered the room. The first was a short bald doctor with the nametag Dr. Chow clipped on his breast pocket. A woman resembling Rose, tiny, fair, and pink-cheeked, followed. She wore a black suit and sported a man's haircut. An elderly woman, wearing a lost and confused expression and a patchwork skirt, denim shirt, and lace-up boots trailed behind them.

Lizbet kept her mother's hand in her grip, but stood.

Nurse Stacy hugged her clipboard to her chest.

"Who are you?" the Rose look-a-like demanded.

"I'm Lizbet. Who are you?"

The woman snorted.

"You're Lizbet?" The elderly woman's hand fluttered near her chest. "So am I. Well, they used to call me that. My name is Elizabeth."

"What I meant was," the carbon copy of Rose said, "what's your relationship to Daugherty?"

Lizbet dropped her mother's hand and went to pick up the elderly woman's. Her skin felt smooth and warm. "I'm Rose's... Daugherty's daughter."

The middle-aged woman snorted again. "Oh, this is just ridiculous!"

Elizabeth blinked. "It's wonderful. A miracle. My daughter has been missing for nearly twenty years. And now she's returned and brought a daughter of her own with her."

The woman took Elizabeth's arm and drew her away from Lizbet. "Mother, be reasonable. We don't know who this is. We can't even be sure this is Daugherty!" She waved an arm over the bed like she was brushing away cobwebs.

"Nonsense, Josie." Elizabeth's eyes gazed into Lizbet's. "How can you doubt this is Daugherty? She looks just like you, except for better."

Which Lizbet thought was a really insulting thing to say, considering her mom's gray skin and bloodless lips.

Josie must have thought so, too. "Mother!" She stomped her high-heel.

"Maternity is easy to validate," Dr. Chow murmured.

Elizabeth gave him a quick scowl. "We don't need to waste our money on unnecessary tests. Of course this is my daughter. She's the spitting image of her sister and her Aunt Connie." Elizabeth peered at Lizbet as if trying to determine her blood pool. "I'm not sure where you sprang from, but knowing Daugherty, I'm sure it will prove to be an interesting story."

"You don't know this girl from Adam!" Josie protested.

"I highly doubt she's from Adam, if you mean the husband of Eve, but the most important thing is she knows where she's from, and she can tell us what Daugherty has been up to these past twenty years."

"I can tell you what I know," Lizbet said, "but you might be disappointed at how little that is." Lizbet stared at Elizabeth. Was this truly her grandmother? Was this Josie, a hostile carbon copy of her mother, her aunt? Did she have family after all, and if so, why would her mom hide from them? Elizabeth, at least, looked harmless.

Elizabeth wiped a tear from her eye. "This is such a miracle..."

"Yes," Josie muttered, sounding much less awe-struck. "Dr. Chow, why don't you tell us my sister's prognosis?"

Lizbet motioned to the chair and Elizabeth sank into it with a grateful but nearly inaudible sigh. It was easy to see her relationship with Josie was strained. Lizbet began to wonder how Rose had fared growing up with Josie.

Rose typically wore her hair loose around her shoulders or tied back with a strip of ribbon. Josie had her hair clipped close to her head. The mannish cut suited her and showed off her strong chin. She wore a black well-tailored suit, dark hose, and two-inch high heels, and she tapped on her phone while the doctor spoke. It took Lizbet a moment to realize Josie was taking notes. This helped Lizbet to not completely hate her.

"So, as you can see, this stage can last for minutes or years," Dr. Chow concluded.

"Years?" Josie's voice cracked. "I'm sure she wouldn't want to remain in this vegetable state for years."

"She's no more a vegetable than I am a fruit," Elizabeth said.

"That's certainly debatable," Josie muttered.

"In fact, I believe that she's listening to us right now." Elizabeth pushed back the pale hair from Rose's forehead.

Josie audibly swallowed.

"I hope so," Lizbet whispered.

"Well then, I hope she wakes up soon so she can answer some questions!" Josie said, frowning at her sister.

"The best thing we can do is keep her comfortable," Dr. Chow said.

"And that includes keeping your conversations positive," Nurse Stacy put in, giving Josie a nasty look. "She has to want to wake up."

Josie rolled her eyes. "Mother, I must get back to work."

"Of course Josie," Elizabeth said. "I think I'll stay here and get to know my granddaughter." She winked at Lizbet. "If that's okay with you."

"How will you get back to the ranch?" Josie asked.

"You can pick me up after work."

"I don't have time for that!"

"Well, then I'll have Perez come and get me."

Josie snorted and looked like she wanted to stomp her high heel again.

Elizabeth waved her hand as if shooing away flies. "Don't worry about me. I'll be fine."

Josie slid Lizbet a suspicious glance. "It's not you I'm worried about," she muttered as she strode out the door. Dr. Chow and Nurse Stacy followed. The room fell silent save the buzzing and beeping of the monitors.

"Why does she hate me when she doesn't even know me?" Lizbet asked, breaking the silence.

Elizabeth blinked at her with clouded green eyes. "She doesn't hate you, child. She hates her life."

"Then why doesn't she change it?"

Elizabeth lifted her eyebrows. "It's not an easy thing to do. Especially when you're scared."

"What does she have to be scared of?"

"The world's a scary place."

"That's what my mother always said, too."

Elizabeth folded her hands in her lap. "Why don't you sit down and tell me about your life with my daughter."

Lizbet glanced out the window and spotted Tennyson sitting in the tree. He flicked his tail, letting her know he had all day. Eventually, Lizbet would need to start worrying about where she would spend the night. She didn't want to leave Queen Anne as long as her mother was there, so going back to the island on her own was an impossibility, but she didn't know how much hotels cost or if they allowed cats.

"Do hotels accept cats?"

"You have a cat?" Elizabeth was clearly surprised by the turn of the conversation.

Lizbet nodded at Tennyson.

Elizabeth twisted to peer at the cat on the other side of the thick glass pane. The two studied each other.

"You and your furry friend can stay with me," Elizabeth announced.

"Do you... Don't you think Josie will mind?"

Elizabeth chuckled. "I'm more concerned about Lucy."

"Who's Lucy?"

"My housekeeper. She's a fussbudget and not very fond of cats. Josie would like to believe that she controls my life, but she doesn't. In fact, Lucy has more say than Josie. Now, why don't we have a nice long chat before we worry about how we're going to get your cat out of that tree?"

Lizbet knew there were plenty of more troublesome things to worry about, but she sat down on a chair opposite Elizabeth and told her everything she thought Elizabeth might find interesting. She did not, however, tell her that

she could talk to animals. Although, that was probably the most interesting thing about her.

Perez drove a beat-up mud-colored Ford double-cab truck to the hospital's wide glass doors. He left it idling while he jumped out, tossed Lizbet's suitcase into the truck's bed, opened the back door for Lizbet and helped Elizabeth into the passenger seat. Lizbet liked him even before he said a word.

By the end of the fourteen-mile drive, she decided that words were not really Perez's thing. Elizabeth jabbered in Spanish while Perez maneuvered through the city traffic, across the bridges, and onto the small two-lane highway that led to Elizabeth's home, filling the stout dark man in on all that had happened that day.

Lizbet hugged Tennyson's basket closer to her chest and tried to hide her fear. She'd never traveled so fast. Leonard's boat didn't have nearly the speed of Perez's truck and besides, there wasn't anything to hit out on the water. But here on Queen Anne's busy streets, Perez could hit many things—cars, motorbikes, people.

Occasionally, Perez would send Lizbet questioning glances through the rearview mirror. She met them with a smile and tried to look harmless. She couldn't blame any of Elizabeth's friends or family for being suspicious of her. She would be, too.

They rounded a hill and Lizbet's breath caught in her throat when the ranch came into view. The sun had yet to completely disappear, but the moon, fat and round, hovered on the horizon. Nestled in a valley of vibrant grass and yellow buttercups sat a white farmhouse with blue trim. The meadow disappeared into a ridge of alders sprouting new green leaves, and a mountain topped with snow sat in the distance. Not far from the house lay a massive red barn. Chestnut-colored horses in all shapes and sizes meandered in the meadow beyond a white split-rail fence. An unfamiliar wave of recognition swept through Lizbet. She felt like she was coming home, although she knew she'd never been here before.

"Your home is beautiful," Lizbet told Elizabeth.

Elizabeth sent her a questioning look. "I would like to see your island. I'm very curious as to where my daughter has been and how she's been living all these years."

"I'd be happy to take you there," Lizbet said.

"Mmm... We'll have to do that. Although, I think I'd like to wait for Daugherty to go with us."

A lump formed in Lizbet's throat, and she swallowed around it. "I'd like that, too."

"In the meantime, you'll stay here with me."

"That's really generous of you," Lizbet said, but she couldn't help thinking that there had to be some reason her mother had cut off contact with her family all these years. If her mom had wanted Elizabeth to be a part of

Lizbet's life, she would have introduced them—right? So why hadn't she?

"I hope that you'll be able to tell me all about my mom before she came to the island," Lizbet said.

"It would be my pleasure."

From her perch on the backseat, Lizbet could do little but study the back of Elizabeth's head. She wished she could read her. Animals were so good at that. They could draw almost instantaneous character assessments. Sure, she knew they had skills she lacked, smell being one of them, but she wished she had some animal instinct right now. Elizabeth looked harmless. Her smile and warmth seemed genuine. And she shared Lizbet's name, making Lizbet think that her mom had probably named her after Elizabeth.

And yet, why the secrecy? Why had her mother been hiding on the island?

Perez steered the pickup through a pair of wide whitewashed gates and pulled up in front of the large brick-red barn with white trim. With Tennyson's basket tucked in her arms, Lizbet climbed from the truck.

Perez already had her suitcase and bag.

"It's not much," Elizabeth said.

But Lizbet heard the pride ringing through Elizabeth's voice. She followed Perez and Elizabeth up the porch steps and through the front door.

Lizbet sucked in a deep breath. The air inside was cooler than outside and smelled faintly of lavender. She

gazed around the room, taking note of the enormous stone fireplace, the floor-to-ceiling windows, and the long stretches of hardwood floors.

"I'll show you to your room," Elizabeth said.

Lizbet nodded without saying a word and trailed after Elizabeth and Perez up the wide staircase. Running her fingers up the railing, she wondered if her mom had touched this banister when she was Lizbet's age. One thing Lizbet had learned from her life on the island and being dependent on the harvest for a living was that things almost always came full circle. A baby is born, the aged die. A seed is planted, nurtured and cared for, but eventually the vine withers and turns brown and brittle before it goes back into the ground, replenishing the earth, making it even more hospitable for future seeds.

Elizabeth paused at the first bedroom on the right and pushed open the door. Faint early stars shone through the windows. A large four-poster bed dominated the room. Lizbet fought back the urge to curl onto it.

Perez set the bags down by the door.

"Thank you, Perez," Elizabeth said. "I'll meet you in the barn in a moment."

Perez nodded and after giving Lizbet another curious glance, he turned and left.

Elizabeth patted Lizbet's arm. "I bet you're exhausted. Why don't you settle in while I go and see if Lucy put any extra leftovers in the fridge?"

Lizbet shook her head. "I'm not hungry." Her stomach was so tied in worry knots, she didn't think she could eat.

"Are you sure?"

"Positive." At the moment, all she wanted to do was curl into a ball and sleep until her mom woke.

Elizabeth must have read the questions in Lizbet's eyes. "You'll meet Lucy's son, Matías, as well. He's been hanging around here his entire life. Lucy homeschool her kids. They're both as smart as whips." Elizabeth cocked her head. "Are you still in school?"

"I've never been to school."

"Homeschooled?"

"I guess you could call it that..." She'd read a ton of books over the years and her mother had taught her simple math, but there had never been anything formal or structured.

Elizabeth blew out a tiny sigh. "Well, I believe in education, and if you're my granddaughter you're going to get one whether you want it or not!"

"Why? What am I going to do with it?"

"What are you going to do without it?"

Lizbet didn't really know how to answer that question. The island was all she knew. Her mother had told her that the world was full of terror and that staying on the island was the only safe choice.

But Lizbet had always wondered. She loved her mom too much to defy or question her, and yet, a secret part

of her had always longed to see the rest of the world. And now she had her chance…

But she couldn't just take advantage of Elizabeth. Even if she was her grandmother, it wasn't right for Lizbet to live at the ranch without paying for something.

Tennyson clearly didn't share her reservations because he jumped out of his basket and stalked about the room, his nose and tail lifting as he inspected their new home.

"It looks like your kitty likes it here," Elizabeth said.

"Of course he does. It's lovely. What's not to like?"

"There's a creature nearby," Tennyson warned.

"Do you have dog?" Lizbet asked Elizabeth.

"No, but Matías has Raphael, a giant Great Pyrenees Mountain dog." Elizabeth smiled. "I'm sure you'll love him."

Tennyson sniffed. *"I'm sure I won't!"*

"Although, I'm not so certain about that guy." Elizabeth nodded at Tennyson.

Lizbet crossed the room, mindful of how her feet sunk into the rich, fat carpet. "It's so nice of you to let us stay here."

The lines around Elizabeth's eyes crinkled and her eyes brightened with unshed tears. "My pleasure." She cleared her throat and blinked twice. The tears disappeared. "Lucy serves dinner at five, so we missed that ages ago, but I'm sure she left us something. If you want to lie down, or look around, I'll leave that up to you. I need to check on Pricilla, she's about to foal, but if you're hungry or if you need anything, you can help yourself to anything in the kitchen."

After Elizabeth left, Lizbet wasn't really sure what to do with herself. She sat down on the bed and Tennyson jumped up beside her.

"Now what?" the cat asked, curling onto her lap.

"I guess we stay here until my mom gets better."

"What if she doesn't?"

"Don't say that. Don't even think it."

"What's this school she talked about?"

Lizbet thought about the books she'd read. Of course things had changed since Jane Eyre went to Lowood Institute, or even since Scout had to be a pork leg in a school play. Curiosity tingled through Lizbet. She wanted to just go and look at a high school. If she could be invisible that would be best, then no one would stare at her, or her clothes, and she could just watch.

"What's that?" Tennyson flicked his tail at a black box with a glassy surface on the wall.

"I'm not sure."

Tennyson padded across the bed and over the nightstand. The black box flashed with light. A two-dimensional man sitting behind a desk showed up on the glass. His lips moved as if he were talking, but he didn't make a sound.

Lizbet was too surprised to scream.

"He's trapped in there," Tennyson said.

"I don't think he can see us." Lizbet sat down on the bed. "This must be a television. I read about them." She cocked her head. "Amazing. He looks so real."

"Is it like a moving photograph?"

"Or a movie. I read about those, too. I think they're just like this, only bigger."

"Why did it turn on?"

"I'm not sure," Lizbet said slowly. She glanced at the nightstand and caught sight of a small black device covered with buttons. It looked a lot like the phone. She picked it up, pressed a button, and girls in bikinis carrying surfboards replaced the man behind the desk. Another button and the screen flicked to a grotesquely disfigured man dressed in rags stumbling down the street while a crowd of teenagers ran away with their arms waving in the air. Another button and a giant purple creature danced around a room with a cluster of children—this, Lizbet decided, was the most terrifying of all. She pushed another button and music flooded the room but the purple monster remained.

"Turn it off!" Tennyson cried.

Lizbet pushed one button after another until the screen faded to black. She plopped onto the bed holding the device between her legs. Tennyson curled up beside her.

"I don't think I like television," Tennyson said, twitching his tail.

A pretty girl with dark hair stuck her head around the door. "Was that you watching Blarney?"

"What's a Blarney?" Lizbet's gaze shot from the device to the television and back to the device. "I thought I was watching a television."

The girl's lips twitched and she stepped into the room. She wore blue jeans and a white lacy shirt and carried a stack of bright white towels that, by contrast, made her skin a richer brown and her lips a deeper red. "I'm Maria, and that purple dinosaur you just saw is Blarney."

"I don't like Blarney."

"That's okay. I don't think anyone does." Maria put the towels down on the dresser, folded her arms, and studied Lizbet with warm chocolate eyes.

"Why would the parents of those children let them play with him? I mean, I know he's not real. He must be a man in a costume fooling those children... It's so wrong."

Maria laughed and flicked her hair over her shoulder. "Your grandmother sent me to see if you'd like something to eat."

Lizbet shook her head. The thought of food made her ill. She felt overwhelmed, tired, and worried about her mom and about her own future. It was as if everything in her life would need to be rewritten. Without her mom, without the island, she didn't know who she was or where she belonged. "I'm okay," she said, although she absolutely was not.

Maria seemed to know Lizbet was lying, but she didn't press her. "I heard about your mom, I'm sorry."

"Yeah, me, too."

"Elizabeth is going to pay me to tutor you in English and social studies. Matías, that's my brother, is going to help you in math and algebra."

"Algebra? What's that?"

Maria laughed again as she turned around to leave. "I know, right? Tomorrow, I'll introduce you to Lincoln Academy. That's the homeschool program I graduated from. Your grandmother wants to know where you are academically. I'll be by around eight."

Maria said goodbye, leaving Lizbet feeling more alone than ever been before. She settled down on the bed and gazed up at the ceiling, wondering about the strange turn of events that had brought her to this place.

A gentle rapping shook the door. Lizbet bounced off the bed to open it. She found a red-eyed Elizabeth standing in the hall with an armful of photo albums.

"I wanted to show you these. I want to introduce you to the Daugherty Westmoor that I knew and loved."

The next morning, Lizbet sat at the breakfast table with Elizabeth. Putting down her spoon, and gazing at the empty cereal bowl, she said, "I think I'm in love with Captain Crunchies."

Elizabeth laughed. "I do believe he's closer to my age than yours, and if so, I get first dibs!"

"Does my mother know about him?"

"Of course. She ate Captain Crunchies every morning for years."

"How could she have possibly stayed away?"

Pain flashed across Elizabeth's expression, and Lizbet immediately regretted her thoughtless words. Before the silence could grow anymore awkward, a knock sounded on the Dutch door. Maria and a dark-haired boy who was clearly her brother stood on the other side of the glass.

Elizabeth pushed away from the table to let them in.

"Elizabeth," Lizbet said, afraid that her time to speak up was about to run out, "it's really kind of you to let me stay here, but—"

Elizabeth pinned her with a steady gaze. "There are no buts! You are my granddaughter. I've been denied you and your mother's company for nearly twenty years. Please say you'll stay!"

"Yes, but... I have to earn my keep!"

"We can talk about that later. Today, my friends are going to introduce you to their online school, and in a few hours, we'll go and visit your mom. We can talk about the conditions of your stay on our drive to Queen Anne. Deal?"

Lizbet tried to make her smile look bright with gratitude, but it felt strained. "Is this school expensive?"

"Hush!" Elizabeth made a zipping motion in front of her lips "I dislike money talk."

"Yes, but—"

"No more buts," Elizabeth said, turning her back on Lizbet so she could throw open the door.

Maria and Matías walked in. Maria was tall, but Matías

was taller. Broad, brown-eyed, he looked like he belonged on the cover of a romance novel. Lizbet immediately knew she was going to enjoy her studies.

"This is my doofus brother." Maria nodded at the hulk standing beside her. "Keep in mind that even though he acts like a know-it-all, I'm actually ten months older. That's important."

Matías responded by shouldering his sister and sending her bouncing against the doorframe.

"Hey!" Maria pushed him back but he didn't even move.

Lizbet grinned, liking Matías immediately.

Chapter Seven

The problem with Baxter was his size. It made him lazy, but it also made Declan mad. It had been much more fun to shoot hoops with Baxter when he didn't have arms and legs like strings of spaghetti. In the last three years, Baxter had sprouted into a monster on the basketball court and an anomaly everywhere else. At the moment, he planted himself under the basketball hoop attached to his garage, snagged the ball from Declan, and casually tossed it in. Declan darted for the rebound and sprinted out of Baxter's considerable wingspan.

"So, you going to Nicole's party tonight?" Baxter asked.

Declan used the back of his hand to wipe the sweat off his forehead. He would have used his shirt, but he'd discarded it about three baskets ago. Baxter, he noticed, hadn't even broken a sweat.

"Yeah. Are you?"

Baxter nodded. "Gina and Nicole are tight."

Declan knew this because his goal was to know everything about Nicole. He tried to look casual as he dribbled the ball forward and back.

"You bringing a digit?" Baxter barely shuffled his feet as Declan bounced around the sports court.

"I thought I'd go single digit," he said, trying not to sound winded.

"Bad move, bud."

Declan caught the ball and held it at his side. "Why do you say that?"

"You like her, right?"

Declan didn't respond and resumed dribbling.

"Chicks like to think they're catching a prize. You got to make them think they're scoring."

It was one thing for Baxter to outplay him on the basketball court—it was another for him to hand out lady-tips. With a burst of speed, Declan plowed into Baxter's sizeable hulk to sink a layup.

"Good one," Baxter said, sounding insultingly surprised.

Declan grunted as Baxter took possession of the ball. "Especially Nicole," Baxter said.

"What does that mean?" Declan tried not to wheeze as he bumped into Baxter.

"Man—if you did that in a game, you'd be benched," Baxter complained.

"This is not a game. It's war." Declan stole the ball and dribbled to the far corner of the sports court.

"Yeah, and Jason's going out with Nicole." Baxter stayed under the basket. "But she's feisty. She likes to win. I know she looks sweet, and everything—"

Declan really didn't want to listen to Baxter spout off about Nicole like he knew her better than Declan did. He bounced the ball to the edge of the court and was about to shoot a three-pointer when—

"Declan!"

The ball dropped at his feet and he spun.

"Mom?"

Dressed in a black pantsuit with a bright coral camisole, Gloria stood beside her idling silver Mercedes. Despite her polished clothes and perfectly coiffed hair, something about her seemed frantic and wrong. Declan wished he could see beyond her dark sunglasses.

He let the ball roll toward Baxter, who also ignored it.

"It's your grandfather," she said.

Baxter raised his eyebrows in a question that Declan didn't know how to answer.

Shrugging, Declan picked up his shirt and headed down the driveway toward the street and the idling car.

"He wants to meet you before..." Gloria took off her glasses to wipe her tears with a rolled-up napkin.

Her red eyes and puffy nose told Declan that she was genuinely upset, which surprised him. He pulled open the car door and slid inside. "What happened?"

"I'm not sure." Gloria repositioned herself behind the wheel. "He just said he's in the hospital and he wants to see you immediately."

Weird. His grandfather had never, to Declan's knowledge, wanted to meet him before. "Why now?"

"Mortality has caught up to him, I guess." She put the car in gear and pulled away from the curb.

"Shouldn't I shower or something?" Declan used his shirt to wipe the sweat off his face.

His mom skated him a quick glance before tousling his hair. "I think you're handsome just as you are, but... maybe." Her face went hard. "Do you have clothes at the house, or do you need to go to your dad's?"

Even though his house was just around the corner, he knew she wouldn't want to go there and risk running into his dad. Baxter thought Gloria avoided his dad because she felt guilty and she didn't like the feeling, so it made her "testy"—Baxter's word. Someday, Declan knew, Baxter would grow up to be a therapist like his mom, even though he would never admit to his constant reading of the people around him. He wondered what Baxter would have to say about Declan's mom's tears over his grandfather.

"I have jeans and a few shirts at your house," Declan told her.

Gloria pressed her lips together and flipped on the blinkers, turning away from John's condo and heading for Godwin's monstrosity. "It'll have to do."

The three hours Lizbet had spent in front of the computer with Maria and Matías had left her both dazzled and bewildered. The world was suddenly much larger than she'd ever imagined. They'd even shown her Wellington boots. Matías had just typed "Wellington boots" into the search engine and suddenly—Boom!—hundreds of images of Wellington boots. Fortunately, the boots only came in a few styles and they were all pretty distinct. Not that she could assume just anyone wearing a pair was responsible for her mom's condition or Wordsworth death, but still it was something.

If only she'd been able to convince the seagulls and crows who had seen the monster to come with her, but the birds were surprisingly territorial and committed to their life on the island.

No one that Lizbet knew of on Elizabeth's ranch wore Wellingtons. Elizabeth herself had said that she didn't know anyone who wore those boots, but she admitted that she really didn't pay that much attention to people's footwear. But now, as they walked through the hospital, Lizbet kept her eyes near the floor. Most of the nurses wore fat white

shoes with thick rubber soles. Some of the girls her age wore sandals like Maria's—Maria had called them flip-flops. Some of the doctors wore paper-like booties over their shoes.

She ran into something. Or someone. A hand reached out and steadied her. She looked up into Declan's face. She found herself comparing him to Matías. They both had dark hair. Declan was tall and lanky, but Matías was solid and square. Matías had brown eyes, Declan's were blue. Declan's skin was a shade pinker, but maybe that was because he was blushing. Was he? And if so, why?

"Hey," he said, "still looking for veterans or Presbyterians?" He held a steaming Styrofoam cup in front of him.

She smiled, despite her sadness. "No. This time I'm looking for Wellington boots."

Her response seemed to surprise him. "Why? What are Wellington boots?"

She told him about the footprints in the cove and how she believed they belonged to the man who had beaten her mom and killed her dog. Compassion flickered in his eyes again.

"Why, hello, Declan," Elizabeth said from behind Lizbet. She had been lingering in Lizbet's mom's room and must have caught up to Lizbet.

"Do you know Declan?" Lizbet asked her grandmother.

"Why, of course. The Westmoors and Forsyths are old family friends," Elizabeth said. She flashed a look

between Declan and Lizbet. "And how do you two know each other?"

"His dog chased Tennyson up a wall," Lizbet told her.

"Interesting..." Elizabeth said.

"Not really," Lizbet said bluntly.

"How's your mom?" Declan asked.

A wave of sadness washed over Lizbet. "The same."

Elizabeth wrapped a comforting arm around Lizbet's waist. "She's in a coma, but the doctors are quite hopeful. And what brings you here?" Elizabeth asked.

"My grandfather wanted to meet me." He bit his lip.

"Does that mean that he hasn't already?" Lizbet asked.

Declan nodded and shrugged, so Lizbet didn't really know what he meant, but Elizabeth seemed to.

"That's wonderful!" Elizabeth exclaimed. "A reconciliation at last, I hope?"

Declan made another noncommittal gesture. "He was sleeping and my mom didn't want to wake him... so we're waiting." He lifted up the cup of coffee. "I've been sent for reinforcements."

"You know, Declan, I've known your grandfather my entire life," Elizabeth said. "I've always felt badly about the rift between him and your mom. It's a shame you didn't get to know him earlier."

"We're trying to change that," Declan said. "I hope there's still time."

"He was always such a pistol!" She chuckled softly. "I

remember when he rode his motorcycle through the halls of the high school!" She sighed. "We all age…"

"But not all of us grow up," a voice behind Lizbet said.

Lizbet turned, but not before she caught sight of a scowl settling between Elizabeth's eyebrows.

"Josie." Elizabeth drew out her name like a sigh. "I would have thought you'd be at work this time of day."

"Late lunch," Josie said, stooping to kiss her mother on the cheek. "I thought I'd drop by and check on my sister."

"Well, that's sweet of you, dear, but sadly unnecessary. I'm afraid she's still the same."

"I'm afraid of that, too," Josie said under her breath. She cast a critical eye at Lizbet.

Lizbet flinched under the steady gaze. Josie, despite her severe hairstyle, square chin, and manly clothes, was almost as beautiful as her sister, Rose. But whereas Rose was soft, her coloring pink, and her gaze tender, everything about Josie was brittle and severe.

Lizbet caught herself. She had to remember that her mom's name was no longer Rose, but Daugherty. It made her mom seem like a stranger.

"Mrs. Westmoor." Dr. Chow approached. He wore a sympathetic smile and carried an electronic tablet. "I'm glad I caught you. If I could have a moment of your time, I'd like to discuss your daughter's care."

"Of course." Elizabeth nodded at Declan and Josie before stepping down the hall to confer with the doctor.

Josie waited until Elizabeth had moved out of earshot before she rounded on Lizbet. Pointing her finger at Lizbet's chest, she narrowed her eyes. "I don't know who you are or what your game is, but I am watching you!"

Lizbet backed up a step, nearly bumping into Declan. "Watching me? That'll be boring... Although, today I did discover the Internet. So, that was cool." And tomorrow Matías had promised to introduce her to Netflix... that seemed worth watching. Still, although she didn't like Josie, she understood her concern. "I know you don't know me, but if you did, you'd understand I don't want to take advantage of your mom. If I had other options, I'd take them."

Josie leaned forward, her words coming out as one hot, rapid breath. "Why don't you just go back to where you came from?"

Lizbet blinked. True, that was an option, but not a very good one. Not a safe one. Sure, she had the company and defense of the animals, but they hadn't been able to protect her mom from a man with size-fourteen Wellingtons.

"I want to be near my mom," Lizbet said in a small voice.

"Of course you do," Declan said.

Josie shot him a venomous glance, her eyes widening when she recognized him. "Gloria's kid..."

"Yeah. I'll tell my mom you said hi," Declan said. "And my stepfather."

"How do you know... her?" Josie tipped her head at Lizbet.

"Lizbet," he emphasized her name, "and I go way back."

Lizbet smiled at the blatant lie.

Josie's gaze darted between them. "How is that even possible?"

"You know what they say, all things are possible with a dog." Declan took Lizbet's arm and steered her down the hall.

"No one says that, right?" Lizbet stumbled to keep up with him.

"Right. But you know Beetle the dog, and I don't know God, who is usually referenced in that context, so it seemed like the right thing say."

"It was a lie."

"Was it? We go way back to yesterday."

Lizbet breathed out a soft laugh.

"I didn't like the way she was talking to you," Declan said, his voice tender.

"I can take care of myself," Lizbet said, but she didn't sound very convincing, even to herself.

"Can you?"

"I want to..."

"We can't go far, or else you'll lose Mrs. Westmoor." He motioned to the coffee cup. "Besides, I have to give this to my mom. Want to meet my grandfather? He's almost as entertaining as your mom."

Lizbet elbowed him. "That's so irreverent."

"I'm glad you think so." He smiled and slid her a quick glance. "You're not like other girls."

"What do you mean?"

"I mean... who uses words like irreverent?"

"I guess I do."

He shook his head as if trying to clear it. "You're not like anyone else I know."

"That's okay, right? I mean, you're not really like anyone else I know, either, but the difference is I don't really know very many people."

"Which means you're unique, but I'm just one of the herd."

"Oh no, you're not a herd animal."

"No? Then what am I?"

"I haven't decided yet. Remember, I don't know you all that well, but I know for sure you aren't a herd animal."

"Am I a predator?"

She sucked in a deep breath. "Maybe... definitely a carnivore."

"You got that right."

"While I'm a herbivore."

"Really? And you sound so proud of it, too..."

"I am. At least I'm not ashamed of it."

"So I can't tempt you with a juicy steak?"

She shook her head.

"How about salmon filet?"

"I don't know... I've never had one, Although, I will eat shell fish."

"Shell fish don't count as meat?"

She felt okay about eating shellfish because they were

so tightlipped and silent—absolutely non-vocal, as were most fish.

"Declan!" Elizabeth hurried toward them, brushing past nurses. "Your mom sent me for you. It's your grandfather!"

Declan cast Lizbet a quick glance, as if asking to be excused.

She squeezed his hand. "You better go."

And after a brief nod, he did.

"No drooling," Baxter whispered. "And you're eye-stalking her."

Declan tore his gaze away from Nicole and stared into his plastic cup as if it had an inscription on the bottom in need of deciphering.

Baxter elbowed him. "Don't be a tree."

"What am I supposed to do?" Declan groaned. "I shouldn't have come..."

"Go and talk to someone."

Tonight, Nicole wore a pair of jeans and a white T-shirt. A thin silver necklace hung around her neck. She was the most beautiful thing he'd ever seen in the flesh.

"But not her," Baxter added.

"Then who?"

"Hey, oh tall ones." McNally, another kid from the basketball team, bumped Declan's shoulder with his. McNally, being a forward, didn't have Baxter's height, but what he lacked in height he made up for in aggression.

Declan and Baxter greeted him in guy-speak, which was mostly grunts.

"What's up, other than your heads?" McNally asked.

"Just trying to socialize Declan," Baxter said.

"Why bother?" McNally asked.

Declan ignored them and returned to Nicole-gazing. The dim light glittered on the silver strand around her neck. She stood in a circle of girls, laughing at something someone said. He strained to hear the conversation but the music's steady thrum and the chatter around the room made it impossible. He quickly counted the people, more than fifty, but only one was interesting to him. He wanted to tell everyone else to pipe down.

"Who is that?" McNally lifted his soda can in the direction of the door.

"The Hernandez family," Baxter said. "They're homeschooled. Matias was on the club soccer team, a midfielder. He's good. Really good. Going to UW on scholarship."

"I know them," McNally cut him off. "But I don't know the boho-chic with them. And I definitely should."

Baxter's eyes widened as he gazed and Declan followed that look to the door.

Lizbet. She looked different, and he tried to decide if it was just because he was seeing her out of context. Although, he had guessed she was about his age, in his mind, she didn't belong at a high school party. He wasn't

sure exactly where she belonged. Her tangle of curls had been tamed and caught back into clips. Her lips were glossy as were her eyes. If her stories were true, this had to be a totally new and different experience for her. Sure, Nicole's party was tame as far as parties went. No keg. No drugs. Parents in the next room... but still, for a girl raised on a deserted island, this had to be a crush of people.

"I don't know who that is." Baxter's tone said he wanted to find out.

"Gina," Declan reminded him.

Baxter shot a fast glance at his girlfriend standing in Nicole's orbit. "Right," he said, sounding resigned.

McNally set down his drink, and used both hands to slick back his straw-colored hair. "Boys, I'm going in."

"Wait!" Declan nearly choked on the word.

"What?" McNally asked.

"I, um, know her." Declan did not want to introduce Lizbet to McNally, but he didn't see how he could avoid it. "She's... not your type."

"Why not?"

"She's been... sheltered. She's not like other girls."

McNally raised an eyebrow. "Sounds intriguing."

"Trust me... she's—a—"

Baxter cut in. "Looks like she's with Hernandez."

Declan's breath caught as he watched Hernandez take Lizbet's hand and lead her to the middle of the room where some people were dancing. Hernandez put one hand on Lizbet's waist and then another.

"I gotta meet her," McNally said. "Tell me about her."

Declan scratched his chin and decided that Lizbet should tell her own stories... and probably not to McNally.

"She doesn't go to East End," McNally said, licking his lips. "I absolutely would have noticed her."

"She's homeschooled," Declan ground out, feeling more and more annoyed. He didn't know why—which bothered him even more. "Dancing's stupid."

That got both Baxter and McNally's attention.

"Don't slam any excuse to handle a girl," McNally said.

Declan grunted. "Just look at it. All those couples—no one is even trying to coordinate with the music. It's really just about touching."

McNally raised his eyebrows. "So?"

"People have been dancing for centuries," Baxter said. "It's a basic mating ritual—even in the animal kingdom."

"Mating ritual... there's a thought I won't get out of my head any time soon," McNally said. "Thanks for putting it there."

Baxter grinned. "You're welcome."

Soda spilled over Declan's hand. He looked down and realized he'd squeezed his cup too hard. Neither Baxter nor McNally seemed to notice—they both had their eyes on Lizbet. He shook his hand and went to find a napkin.

Nicole met him at the dining room table. "Hey, Declan, thanks for coming!" She gave him a quick hug. Her hair smelled of apple-scented shampoo. He inhaled sharply.

He looked at the table loaded with chips, pizza, bowls of candy, and a giant tub full of soda cans. "Are we celebrating something, or is this get-together just because?"

She winked at him. "It's definitely a celebration, but I can't tell you why yet."

"I'm not the only one not in on the secret, right?"

"I think you'll like the surprise."

She was wrong. He hated surprises. But he really liked the way her eyes glistened. He turned when someone touched his arm.

Lizbet.

She looked good. Foreign. Gypsy. In comparison, she made Nicole seem bland and borderline boring.

"Hi there, I'm Chad McNally." McNally bounced to Declan's side, making Declan realize McNally must have been lurking and waiting for an opportunity to pounce.

"Lizbet, this is Nicole Gunner." Declan pointedly ignored McNally.

"I'm Lizbet..." She smiled at Nicole and took McNally's outstretched hand.

Declan wondered if she was trying to decide what her last name was. He also wondered when—and if—McNally was going to release her hand.

"Thanks for letting me crash your party," Lizbet said. "Matías said you wouldn't mind."

"The more the merrier, I always say," McNally put in.

"I've never heard you say that," Declan growled.

"The bigger the better, I always say." Baxter referred to his size as he wedged himself into the circle.

"Don't listen to these goons," Declan said.

"Where are you from?" Nicole asked.

"San Mateo Islands," Lizbet answered.

"All of them?" Nicole asked.

Declan thought that was a stupid question, which surprised him. Nicole had been in all of his GATE classes since grade school. She rarely got anything wrong. But she clearly wasn't getting Lizbet.

And, if he could help it, neither was McNally.

"No, it's just Blackstone is so small not very many people have heard of it."

"Do you have to take a ferry?" McNally asked.

"She's not taking you there," Baxter said.

"Hahaha," McNally said, jabbing on elbow into Baxter's side.

Baxter didn't even flinch.

"Private boat," Lizbet said, flashing Declan a quick glance. "Unless you catch a ride with the postman."

McNally and Baxter laughed as if she'd said something worthy of Saturday Night Live. Nicole smiled, while Lizbet looked slightly confused.

Across the room, Matías watched them while a kid from the soccer team talked and waved his hands. After a few minutes, Declan watched Matías excuse himself weave his way through the crowd.

"There you are," Matías said to Lizbet, placing a territorial hand on her shoulder.

"Matías, you must know Nicole," Lizbet said, "but do you know the others?"

Matías nodded at them and bumped fists with Baxter.

"I've known Declan the longest," Lizbet said. "We go back."

"Way back," Declan corrected her.

"Really?" Baxter and McNally asked at the same time.

Declan shrugged and tried not to look smug.

Lizbet gave him a steady gaze, which he read as *who's the liar now?* He flinched and looked away.

The music suddenly stopped and a bell chimed as Mr. Gunner called for everyone's attention. He was a beige man with thinning hair who tried to look younger than his years. He stood in front of the fireplace and motioned for everyone to quiet down. "Hey, first of all, I want to thank you all for coming tonight, and second, we have an announcement." He waved for Nicole to join him. Wrapping an arm around her shoulders, he pulled her close. "We're so proud of Nicki! She's the brightest star in our family, and we're not surprised that others have recognized her brilliance." He raised his plastic cup. "Ladies and gentlemen, I give you Nicole Gunner, soon to be a freshman at Duke University!"

Nicole caught Declan's gaze as the implications raced through him. They were both going to Duke. Jason, he

knew, had a football scholarship to Washington State. Declan and Nicole would be going to Wake Forest, South Carolina, while Jason would be going to Pullman, Washington. Nicole and Jason would be a continent apart.

That should have made Declan happy. He tried to decipher his own feelings—which, he decided, was a Baxter sort of thing to do, and therefore pointless. While everyone around him clapped and looked happy for Nicole—except Jason, who wore a shell-shocked expression and phony smile—Declan excused himself.

Outside, away from the crush of bodies, the girls' perfume, the boys' cologne, and the steady beat of the strange music, Lizbet sucked in a deep breath of the warm moist night air. Directly outside the glass doors, couples lounged on chaises and against the railing of a deck wrapping around the house. Lizbet found solitude around the corner. Here, the night was darker, the moon lower, and even the stars seemed brighter.

She listened to the sound of nocturnal animals hiding in the forest trees bordering the manicured lawn. An owl hooted at a fox in the underbrush, while an opossum commented on the warm weather and predicted a summer heat wave. Another sound, this time a human one, caught her attention.

Tucked in the shadows, Declan was hunched on a step where the deck met the lawn. She wondered if he wanted to

be alone. Her gaze must have drawn his attention, because he turned. His eyes widened when he saw her.

"Are you hiding?" she asked.

"I could ask you the same thing," he said. "How's your mom?"

"The same. How's your grandfather?"

"I don't know." He shrugged. "He was finally awake, but out of it. Completely delirious. He didn't know either my mom or me. The next time we went back, he was asleep again."

"I'm sorry," she said.

"Don't be. I don't even know him. That's weird, right?"

She laughed softly. "I'm beginning to realize that I'm not a good judge of what is and isn't weird."

He turned away, hiding his eyes, letting her know that he probably agreed with her. "So how do you know Matías?" he asked, changing the subject.

"He's my tutor."

"Ah."

"Turns out my grandmother is an advocate of formal education."

"And you're not?"

She shrugged. "I haven't had any, so I'm not in a position to say."

"Wow. What do you want to do with your life?"

"That's a loaded question." She sucked in a deep breath and sat beside him on the step. "Right now, all I want to do is find out who beat my mom and why."

"No clues?"

"Just a man with size-fourteen Wellington boots."

"How do you know you're looking for a man?"

She couldn't very well tell him that the gulls had seen the assailant. "Not very many women have that size of shoe."

"Maybe it the boot print was a decoy."

"Maybe..." she said slowly.

"Anyway, you can't condemn all men with big feet."

She looked at his really long and skinny feet.

He laughed softly. "Yes... I wear a size-fourteen shoe. But so does Baxter and a couple of other guys on the basketball team."

She really wished she had gotten a better description of the man from the gulls. Sadly, gulls, despite all their noise, weren't great conversationalists. They were mostly concerned about their next meal.

She studied him. "You do have the right hair color."

"How do you know his hair color?"

She scrambled for a lie. "I found a dark strand of hair in the hall."

"You have dark hair," he pointed out.

"Yes, but mine's long and curly. This was short and straight."

He raised his eyebrows. "You're a regular Sherlock."

"But I don't smoke a pipe."

"And you're better looking than Benedict Cumberbatch"

"Thank you, but who is that?"

He rocked back as if surprised. "You've never watched Sherlock?"

"I've read most of Conan Doyle's work." She shook her head. "But I've never watched anything... Matías did introduce me to YouTube today. I love it."

He stood and took her hand. "Come on."

"Where are we going?"

"To watch Sherlock, of course."

She cast a backward glance at the house. "I can't just leave. I came with Matías. He's probably wondering where I am."

"Let's go find him. He can come, too."

"Where are we going?" she repeated.

"To my mom's house." He nodded at flickering lights through the trees. "She lives down the street."

"And you don't?"

"No. I live with my dad, mostly, but I'm at my mom's a lot. She won't mind. In fact, I'm pretty sure she's not home."

About ten people ditched Nicole's party to watch Sherlock. Lizbet sat on the sofa between Declan and Matías trying to enjoy the show, but she found it really hard to concentrate because as they had entered a back door and passed through a small hall she'd spotted a large pair of Wellington boots standing beside an umbrella stand and a giant snoring Husky on the kitchen rug.

From Declan's Research
"I want to realize brotherhood or identity
not merely with the beings called human,
but I want to realize identity with all life,
even with such things as crawl upon earth."
—Mohandas Gandhi

Chapter Eight

As Lizbet lay in her bed beneath Elizabeth's thick quilt, she couldn't help shivering despite the warmth. Thinking that Declan might be the man responsible for her mom's coma and Wordsworth's death left her cold. And worried. And scared.

"You have to take him to the island," Tennyson said. *"The gulls can identify him."*

"How can I do that?" Lizbet pulled the quilt tighter around her shoulders, trying to shut out the breeze blowing in through the open window.

"Easy. Tell him you need to pick up a few things and you don't want to go alone."

"But why him? Don't you think he'll wonder?"

"Probably. But he might also be flattered."

"Oh." The realization that he might think of her that way paralyzed her. But why not? He was a boy. She was a girl. She thought back on how it had felt to be sitting beside him on the back deck. She'd liked it. But she'd liked it a whole lot less when they'd sat side by side on the couch after she'd seen the boots and her suspicions had soured her mood. "How can I go alone? What if he's the murderer?"

"Invite Matías, too."

She snorted. "I can't do that." There had been an undercurrent that she couldn't define running between the two boys. "I know, I'll ask Elizabeth to come. She said she wanted to see the island."

"Won't Declan wonder why you invited him?" Tennyson asked.

"Yes. Probably." Lizbet settled back against the pillows. "Maybe I'll think of something in the morning." She tried to sleep, but all her thoughts were grim. When she finally did sleep, her dreams were darker than her thoughts.

Gloria raised her eyebrows the next morning when Declan stumbled into the kitchen.

"You don't mind that I stayed here last night, right?" Declan mumbled, trying to wake up.

"No, of course not." Gloria smiled as she raised her coffee mug. "Does this mean you'll be coming to church with us?"

Again? Inwardly, Declan groaned. He plucked a muffin off the counter, dropped into a kitchen chair, and wondered about his stepfather. The thought of Godwin in his mother's bed made him sick. He picked the raisins out of his muffin and collected them onto a napkin, feeling less hungry than he had when he'd sat down.

His mom's phone rang and she glanced at the screen. "It's Mrs. Westmoor," she said, sounding surprised.

He half listened to his mom's side of the conversation. "I think he'd be happy to," Gloria said, looking pointedly at Declan.

He frowned, trying to read her.

"You don't need to rent a boat. We have one. Yes, Declan can drive. He's insured." Gloria paused and put her hand over the receiver. "Do you have plans today?" she whispered.

"Why?" he mouthed back, but, by this point he had a guess.

"I think this just might be his ticket to avoiding church," Gloria said into the phone.

Declan smiled and picked up his muffin, his appetite returning as he thought about spending a day with Lizbet, a boat, and an island.

Declan's shoes were the first thing she looked at. Sandals. Brown. Leather. Not Wellington boots. They'd

met at the marina. The gulls flying overhead jabbered about a box of donuts someone had left unattended near the gear shack. Of course these gulls didn't know her, her mom, or Wordsworth.

Declan shook Elizabeth's hand and grinned at Lizbet.

Please don't let him be the murderer, she thought.

Lizbet scanned the air, searching for a familiar seagull or pelican. A few sea lions lounged on a rock protruding from the glassy Sound. They lifted their heads and waved their fins as Declan, Elizabeth, and Lizbet passed, but Lizbet didn't recognize them. Of course the animals outnumbered the people close to two to one. That number would skyrocket if one included the insects. But no one ever included insects, and very few people even counted the animals.

Declan's dad's speedboat was small and dingy-white with a bright yellow cover canopy—nothing like the monster yacht the murderer had sailed to Blackstone Island.

Elizabeth took the chair beside the driver's seat while Lizbet took the backbench. Homesickness washed over her as they moved through the harbor toward the Haradan Strait. As the boat picked up speed, water sprayed through the air, and Lizbet held onto her hat.

Gulls wheeled overhead, calling out greetings. A pod of dolphins cut through the water. Lizbet recognized them immediately. They often hung around Blackstone Island and had frequently brought her news of the local goings-

on. Dolphins, unlike most animals, loved gossip. The pod chattered around them, easily matching the speedboat's pace.

"Have you seen a boat as fine as this?" Lizbet asked Doggie, one of the brighter dolphins. What she really was asking was, *Have you seen this boat before*, but that wasn't something she could ask in front of Declan.

"Often enough." Doggie chattered beside the boat's prow. *"The owner likes to fish. He leaves our herring and squid alone, though."*

Declan looked over his should. "It's like you're conversing."

"The dolphins are more like gossips than they are conversationalists." Lizbet laughed while she spoke, trusting that Declan wouldn't take her seriously.

Declan's lips twitched. "They're gossips, huh? What do they tell you about me?"

Lizbet sucked in a deep breath and rose to the challenge. "So Doggie, what can you tell me about Declan?"

Declan's eyebrows shot up. "His name is Doggie?"

Doggie jabbered a long-winded response.

Lizbet interpreted. "He says you've been coming here since you were little."

Declan's expression clouded. "Wait. What? He didn't really say that, right?"

Lizbet laughed again. "What do you think?"

The ride to the island was shorter than Lizbet remembered. Her trip to Queen Anne with Leonard

had seemed an eternity, but now when worry and fear no longer hounded her, the boat skimmed through the calm Sound, and it seemed as if they pulled into familiar waters in a short time. Although, she'd only been away a few days, Lizbet's heart warmed as she guided Declan toward the cove.

The gulls called out a welcome. She smiled and waved at them, trying to look natural. While Declan was preoccupied with tying up the boat, Lizbet pulled out the piece of bread she'd tucked in her bag. Before jumping off the boat, she showed it to the gulls. They eagerly followed her to a thicket of woods. While tearing the bread to bits, she asked the gathered gulls in a hushed tone, "Tell me quickly, is this the man who beat my mother and killed Wordsworth?"

"Lizbet!" Elizabeth's voice floated through the trees. "Now where did that girl go?"

Lizbet couldn't hear Declan's response.

"Coming!" Lizbet called back. "Quick! I need to know," Lizbet whispered to the gulls.

"It's really hard to distinguish human faces," Gilbert said.

"You know mine," Lizbet hissed.

"But we've known you for years," Goosey complained.

"He does have dark hair," Gilbert said.

"But this time he didn't bring that large creature."

That's right, there had been a dog. Someone had called the dog "wolfish." Her thoughts went back to the husky at Declan's mom's house.

"Just tell me it's not him," Lizbet whisper-yelled.

"Okay, it's not him," Gilbert said.

"Is it really not him, or are you just saying that?" Lizbet demanded.

"There's no pleasing you," Gilbert complained. *"You tell me what to say, I do so, and now you're angry."*

Lizbet took a deep breath and fought to keep her voice steady. "I'm not angry."

"Then why aren't you giving us the bread?" Goosy asked.

Lizbet looked down at her hand and realized that she had stopped divvying out the bread. The gulls flapped around her as she ripped it into pieces.

Gilbert gobbled up a piece. *"You know, I don't think it was him."*

Goosy bobbed her head. *"I can't be sure, but maybe I'd know if there was more bread."*

Lizbet threw the remaining bread on the ground and stomped away, thinking that the whole trip had been a waste. She changed her mind as soon as she spotted Declan. He stood at the water's edge, the light reflecting off his dark hair, his bright blue eyes searching for her, and his smile warming her when he caught sight of her.

"Where'd you go?" Elizabeth demanded.

"My dog. I buried him just over there. I wasn't able to shovel a very deep hole and I've been worried about animals digging him up. I know it sounds gruesome, but..."

Compassion flooded Elizabeth's expression.

"I just had to check," Lizbet added.

"Is everything okay?" Declan asked.

She nodded. "The grave looks exactly as I left it. No one's been here, as far as I can tell." She gestured toward the house. "We lived just over that hill. Come on, I'll show you the cottage."

Declan took Elizabeth's elbow and guided her up the path while Lizbet followed. Mice skittered through the tall grass.

"Welcome home," they chittered.

Lizbet could only smile in return.

They crested the hill. The cottage, overrun with ivy, looked desolate, tired, and empty.

Elizabeth paused, sadness in her eyes. "This is where you lived?"

Lizbet nodded.

"What would make Daugherty hide this way for so long?" Elizabeth asked.

"She thought the world a scary place," Lizbet said.

"But why?" Elizabeth asked. "She'd always been such a happy and carefree child."

"But she wasn't a child when she came here, right?" Declan asked.

"Not much older than you," Elizabeth said.

Lizbet skated Declan a glance, wondering how he would take being called a child. He ran his hand through his hair, caught Lizbet's gaze, and gave her a sheepish smile.

"Come on," Lizbet said, "I'll show you inside. I know it must be strange to you, but we were, mostly, happy here."

But the front door wouldn't budge.

"That's strange," Lizbet said, leaning against it. "It's never stuck before."

"It's probably locked," Declan said, brushing her aside so he could give it a try.

"But why? Who? I didn't lock it."

A squirrel ran along a branch of a nearby maple tree. *"Men in uniform,"* he chattered.

"A back door, possibly?" Elizabeth suggested.

"If someone locked the front door, it makes sense they'd lock the back," Declan put in. They tromped around the house anyway, trying all the doors and windows.

"Mmm..." Lizbet considered her options. She didn't want to break a window. "The root cellar has a trap door!"

She led them to the wide plank-like doors lying just a few inches off the ground. Lizbet pulled on the handle and the door gaped open exposing a hole about four feet deep with only a few potatoes and onions lying on the dirt floor.

"A root cellar," Declan murmured.

"It's empty—mostly—now because it's spring. In the fall, this is full of—"

"Don't tell me, let me guess," Declan said, his voice full of laughter. "Root vegetables."

Lizbet nodded. "And bottles of blackberry wine. See the cubby door? That leads to the cellar."

"Blackberry wine?" Elizabeth asked.

"Yes, Daugherty... the other one—although, I now wonder if that was really her name, made it. Years ago, Rose had a successful business that she sold..." She paused as realization dawned. "It wasn't my mother's business, because my mother wasn't Rose, like I thought. Rose, who I thought was named Daugherty, was the one with the wine business." She shook herself. "There are papers and documents in the house. I'll show them to you. They should answer some questions."

Lizbet dropped into the hole. To her surprise, Declan climbed in after her.

"You didn't think I was going to let you have all the fun, did you?" he asked, wiping his hands on his shorts.

He stood close enough for her to feel his warmth. She shivered at his nearness.

"I think you two have a very different idea of fun than me," Elizabeth said." I'm more of a front door sort of gal."

"We'll meet you there," Lizbet said.

Stooping, she pushed open the cubby door that led to the basement and jumped through.

"For being paranoid, your mom lacked certain basic security measures," Declan said. He barely fit through the door.

The cellar had stone walls, a cement floor, and a ceiling made of wooden beams and planks. A small window bordering the ceiling let in filtered light. Lizbet stopped,

sickened, when she spotted a large red stain on the floor. She put her hand over her mouth to keep from gagging.

"Is that... blood?" Declan asked. He put a steadying hand on her back.

Lizbet nodded. "I think so."

"Your mom?"

"Probably Wordsworth, my dog." She'd mopped after moving and burying him, but she hadn't thought about his blood dripping through the floorboards.

He touched her elbow. "Lizbet, I'm so sorry."

"Yeah, me, too." She straightened her shoulders and pushed toward the rickety wooden stairs. A stream of light shone beneath the door that separated the basement from the rest of the cottage. With one had on the wooden rail, she climbed, hyper-aware of Declan close behind.

The kitchen looked just as she'd left it. A couple of teacups on the dish drain, hand towels folded over the oven's door handle, bundles of herbs hanging to dry near the window. A faint odor of rosemary filled the air. Lizbet inhaled deeply—it smelled of home. She wavered on her feet, rocked by overwhelming homesickness.

Declan put his arm around her waist. He didn't try to hold her or pull her close. He was just there. Solid. Warm. Lizbet closed her eyes and tried to steady herself.

Knocking sounded at the front door. Lizbet pulled away from Declan to let Elizabeth in.

She had straightened up the living room before leaving, even though, according to her mystery novels, this was a

crime scene and therefore should have been undisturbed, but now that she'd brought Elizabeth and Declan, she was glad. She didn't want them to think any less of her mom than they already did. She wanted them to know that she and her mom had created a nice home. They had lived in isolation and maybe it had been a shade primitive according to today's standards, but not squalor.

"Let me show you the office and the things I found in the safe." Lizbet directed Elizabeth and Declan through the front hall to the small room. Everything looked exactly as she'd left it. The desk tidy, the books neatly lined up on the shelves, the room seemed to be caught in a holding pattern, waiting for Lizbet and her mom to return.

Lizbet went to the shelves and pulled out the books in front of the safe. She spun the combination on the lock and it clicked open.

The safe was empty. All of the papers Lizbet had found earlier gone. She felt as if someone had punched her in the gut, and she rocked back on her heels, bumping into Declan who peered over her shoulder.

"I take it that you expected to find something," he said.

"The last time I checked, this was full of legal documents, tax forms, and receipts. Most of what I found made little sense to me. Except I learned that before I was born, Rose had a wine business. I thought it was my mom's because I thought that was my mom's name. What else was I supposed to think?" She turned to Elizabeth.

"I was hoping you could help me put the puzzle pieces together, but now..."

"Should we call the police? Report a break-in?" Declan asked.

Lizbet sighed. "I don't know. They already suspect me..."

"Nonsense. Of course we tell the police!" Elizabeth dug into her bag and pulled out a cell phone. "Only I don't get service."

Declan also pulled out his phone and after a quick glance said, "Neither do I."

Lizbet held up her finger. "There's a phone here... or at least there was." She went to the cupboard.

"What a remarkable place for a phone," Elizabeth said.

"I think she didn't want me to find it," Lizbet said.

"Well, it was awfully clever of you to do so," Elizabeth said.

Lizbet bit her lip thinking of that awful day, wishing she could admit she'd had help. "I was desperate."

"Of course you were." Elizabeth picked up the phone. A satisfying ringtone answered. "Let me handle the police," Elizabeth said. "Why don't you show Declan around?"

Outside, Lizbet took a deep breath. She'd missed this. The quiet. The sun on her skin. The breeze whispering through the trees.

"It's like a different world here," Declan said. "No traffic noise, no people... just us."

"I think my mom felt that way, too."

"How did she do it? How could someone completely disappear off the grid?"

Lizbet led him to the garden. The seedlings had sprouted another couple of inches. Little white blossoms covered the tomato plants. The beans and peas were nothing more than spindly vines climbing the trellis her mom had made from fallen branches. "We grew most of our own food."

Declan stared at the garden as if it were a science project. Lizbet laughed at the expression on his face.

"I think the real question isn't how we managed to live off the grid, but why did my mom choose this? What was she afraid of?"

"Who said she was afraid? Maybe she just liked the isolation."

"I think that maybe she grew comfortable with it, but I don't think it was a choice she made lightly. According to Elizabeth, Daugherty was an outgoing, happy person.

They tramped through the tall grass, following the path that led to the woods. When they reached the trees' heavy canopy, the wavy grass turned to ferns. Lizbet stopped in front of a huckleberry bush. "It'll be a hot summer," she said.

"How can you tell?" Declan asked.

"Just look at all the blossoms on the huckleberry bush." Her mouth watered at the thought of the tart berries and another wave of homesickness crashed over her. Where would she be when the huckleberries bloomed? Would her mom still be in the hospital? Were there even huckleberries on Elizabeth's ranch? Instinctively and without knowing why, she reached for Declan's hand.

"Come on," she said. "I want to show you Daugherty's wine shack."

"Rose," he reminded her. "It was Rose's wine shack." He didn't resist when she pulled him deeper into the woods, nor did he drop her hand when they reached the shanty.

"This is where Daugherty made blackberry wine. I'm not a hundred percent sure, but I think the wine is how Daugherty supported herself... and us."

This time Declan didn't correct her, so she did it herself. "I don't know what else to call her." Lizbet's mood sank. "She died when I was little... it's strange, isn't it, that it still makes me sad?"

"Not really. Your world was so small, anyone, especially someone that you were fond of, would have been a giant loss." Declan squeezed her hand. "Do you know how she died?"

Lizbet gazed at the weather-beaten hovel. A light smattering soft green moss covered the mellow silver wood. The door hung ajar and the air inside sparkled with flying dust motes. A slight breeze carried the faint odor of pungent berries mingled with the scent of pine. For just a moment, Lizbet caught a memory of Daugherty, small and dark, bustling around a steaming vat of boiling berries. Lizbet blinked and the memory faded.

"No. I understood death because of the animals, but I didn't watch her die," Liz said. "One day she was here, the next she was gone."

"Wow. And then it was just you and your mom."

"And the animals."

"You keep saying that, as if they're people."

"Well, they're not people, but they are here." She waved her hand at the woods.

Declan looked up at a squirrel watching him from a cedar tree. "What do you mean you understood death because of the animals?"

"Their life expectancy is so much shorter than ours. And their world is, in some ways, harsher. And simpler. I watched the animals, pets and friends, die."

"But it's not the same as watching a person die."

"Isn't it?"

"Animals aren't people."

"You keep saying that. You're about to lose your grandfather, a man you've never met. Which will hurt you more—his death, or the death of your dog?"

"I get what you're saying, but—"

"Animals have spirits—the same as us."

"What do you mean by 'spirits'?"

"They hurt, they mourn..."

Declan smiled and shook his head.

"Just because they can't share their thoughts doesn't mean they don't have any."

"Animals live by instinct. They're bred to survive. They can't reason..."

"They might not always be reasonable, but people aren't always reasonable, either." She folded her arms as if to

protect herself from Declan's hurtful words. She knew he wasn't being intentionally callous, he just didn't understand, and she didn't know if she had the ability to make him see that animals weren't the mindless creatures he supposed.

"True, but..."

"In fact," she persisted, "I could argue that the animals' motives are much more clear and honest than most peoples."

"I think you'd have a hard time explaining that to a water buffalo when he's being chased by a hungry lion." He gazed up at the squirrel and addressed him. "How about you there? What are your motives?"

"At this time of year, he's probably thinking that his store of acorns is low. He's wondering if this year's crop of nuts and seeds will last him through the winter. Spring has just started and he's already worried about the next snow."

"Are you a squirrel whisperer?"

She elbowed him. "Sometimes I feel like I know animals better than people."

"I get that. I do, but I disagree that animals have souls."

"Everything has a soul," Lizbet said, looping her hand around Declan's arm and pulling him along the path. She didn't want to argue with him, but she also wanted him to know he was wrong.

"Everything?" He walked beside her.

She nodded. "Everything not man made."

"So anything manmade is evil?"

"I didn't say that."

"You also didn't describe what you mean by soul. What do you think, exactly, is a soul?"

"I'm inside my body, but I'm not my body... the me that makes me *me* lives independent of my body."

"I disagree."

She stopped, paralyzed by his assertion. "You disagree? Really? How can anyone disagree with that?"

"How can you believe in souls?"

"Everyone does."

"Lizbet, listen to yourself. You've really only known one person in your entire life..." He faced her.

She wanted to wipe the smug expression off his face with a leaf from a stinging nettle. "B-But Whitman—"

"The poet?"

"Yes! Leaves of Grass—"

He tugged on her arm, leading her back to the house. "He was a poet. He wrote fiction for money. His word wasn't—isn't—gospel."

"What about the Bible?"

"Do you believe in the Bible?"

"Of course. Everyone does."

He shook his head. "No. Everyone absolutely does not."

"Really?" This was a new, disturbing thought. "Then how do they know right from wrong? What provides a moral compass?" When her mom had told her about evil men and greedy women, Lizbet had just assumed that these were people who knew right from wrong, but had simply chosen the wrong versus the right.

"What moral compass?"

"Everyone has a moral compass..." Her words trailed away as she realized how naïve she must sound. "Don't they?"

"No."

"You sound so sure. How can you know that?" It had never occurred to her that maybe some people didn't know, or care, about right and wrong. "Everyone has a conscience, right? That voice in your head that helps makes your decisions..."

"No. There's no voice in your head."

"There's definitely a voice in my head..."

He laughed. "That's the definition of schizophrenia."

She pressed her lips together, trying not to be upset.

He wrapped an arm around her shoulder and gave her a friendly hug. "I'm sorry. I didn't mean to upset you."

"I think everyone has a voice in their head. Some people," she skated him a dark look, "might chose to ignore it."

"Hey, I'm not a bad person."

"How do you know? What makes someone good or bad? If you don't believe in the Bible, or an inner moral compass—how can you know if you're bad or good? Are the words good and bad even relevant?"

He chuckled. "Wow. You're deep. You should be a philosophy major."

"What good would that do?"

"Didn't we just establish that there is no good or bad?"

She blew out a frustrated breath. "I want to help the world be a better place. That's *good*." She emphasized the word.

He bumped her with his hip. "That I agree with."

"What do you want to do?"

"Go to medical school. Help people."

"See? You're a good person, too."

"If you say so."

"You also have a voice in your head."

"No."

"Yes."

"I'm not schizoid."

"That's debatable," she said in a huff.

He grinned.

"There you two are!" Elizabeth stood on the porch, waving at them. "Are you ready to go?"

Although, she knew she didn't want to stay on the island by herself, the thought of leaving made Lizbet ill. She felt more solid here, more grounded, more herself. It was easy to lose track of all that she believed when she was on the mainland. Maybe when her mom got better, she'd feel more stable and solid.

She cast Declan a quick glance. Did others share his way of thinking? Was her mother's religious training considered odd and outdated by the rest of the world? Who could answer this?

Her thoughts went to her mom. She missed her with a lonely ache. Images of her mom still, lifeless, and pale in the bleak hospital room flashed in her mind. Somehow she had to revive her.

"I need to get some books from my mom's office," Lizbet told Declan. "Do you mind helping me?"

With Declan following close behind, she went into the living room. Suddenly, she saw the room through his eyes, and she wondered what he would think of the towers of books, the framed homemade art lining the walls, and the loopy crocheted afghan draped over the sofa. It probably looked primitive and homespun to him, but to her it was home. She hated to leave again, but she knew she couldn't stay here alone. Bracing her shoulders, she headed for the office. "I want to pick up my mom's books on herbology."

"Herbology?"

She shot him a dark glance. "Don't tell me you don't believe in herbology."

"I've just never heard it called that."

"Well, now you have," she said, aware that her words sounded clipped and defensive.

She found the books she wanted and piled them in her arms. When Declan moved to take them from her, she shrugged away from him. Maybe it was dumb, but she felt like he didn't deserve to hold them as long as he was skeptical.

They met Elizabeth on the porch, made sure all the doors and windows were still locked, and headed for the boat. Along the way, Elizabeth prattled on about her discussion with the police. They didn't have any leads, but if they still suspected Lizbet, Elizabeth didn't mention it.

Declan let out a moan when they reached the boat. "The keys."

"What?" Lizbet asked.

"They're gone."

Chapter Nine

one?" Elizabeth and Lizbet asked at the same time. "They must have fallen out of my pocket."

"Maybe when you climbed into the root cellar?" Lizbet asked.

He cocked his head, considering. "Seems the most likely."

"Come on, let's go," Lizbet said, resigned to retracing their steps.

"Do you two youngsters mind if I wait here?" Elizabeth asked, looking hot and tired.

Concern flitted through Lizbet as she placed the books down on a boat seat and carefully draped a tarp over them, making sure they were well tucked in and would stay dry on the drive home. "Maybe you should wait in the house. This may take us a while."

"If you don't mind, I'd rather rest on the boat," Elizabeth said.

Declan's shoulders slumped, but he followed Lizbet up the hill and pulled open the root cellar doors.

They both peered into the hole but saw nothing except the few rotting potatoes that had been there earlier.

A squirrel in a nearby tree chattered at them.

"You don't know where the boat key went to, do you?" Lizbet asked the squirrel.

The squirrel let loose a string of odd chirping noises.

Lizbet hid her grin and followed the squirrel's direction. She spotted the key hiding in the tall grass. She pointed it out to Declan, but moments before she reached it, a crow swooped down and scooped it up.

"Hey!" Lizbet called after it.

"Give those back," Declan demanded.

"But it's shiny and pretty," the crow cawed, fluttering his wings and hovering above them.

"Do you have anything shiny?" Lizbet whispered to Declan.

"Why?" Declan pulled out a handful of coins.

"Crows like shiny objects." She plucked out sparkly quarter and a lackluster dime. "They're shallow that way."

"Hey! I heard that!" the crow squawked.

Lizbet held out her hand, showing him the coins. "We need the keys."

"But we don't want you to go," the crow cawed. *"It's empty without you here."* He lifted his beak in the air. *"I'm deeply insulted that you think I could be bought."*

"It's so weird," Declan said, shaking his head. "It's like he's actually talking to you."

Lizbet flashed Declan a glance to make sure he didn't actually believe that she could communicate with the crows.

"Maybe if you had some bread," Declan suggested.

"I think bread is a good idea."

"Give me the keys!" Lizbet growled.

"All right, no need to be huffy." The crow dropped the keys at her feet.

"Thank you," Lizbet said.

"When will you be back?" the crow asked.

It felt mean not to answer, but after sliding another look at Declan's confused expression, Lizbet pressed her lips together and hurried toward the boat and Elizabeth.

Neal's Nursery opened every morning at seven. Declan, of course generally missed the early shift because of school, but since it was spring break, he was there bright and early. He picked up his hose and began the task of spraying down the cement floor while Mr. Neal chatted with his plants, wiped their shiny leaves, and deadheaded the spent blooms. And while Declan believed in talking to plants almost as much as he believed in arguing with crows—which was not at all—he had to admit that Mr. Neal's plants looked healthy and happy.

And Lizbet and that crow?

And not just the crow... there had been some sort of vibe between her and that squirrel as well. Vibe? He didn't believe in vibes, healing crystals, vampires, or anything that he couldn't see, hear, or touch. Which, an ornery voice in his head told him, ruled out atoms, protons, and nuclear fission. Those are different, he argued with the voice. Those had scientific backing. Then he remembered he didn't believe in voices in his head. He aimed his hose at a lilac bush, taking care not to spray the newly formed blossoms, while shutting out the voice.

"Declan!" His mom dressed in a gray pantsuit and a silky pink shirt hurried toward him. In her real estate broker-wear, she looked out of place among the plants, bags of soil, and bird feeders. "It's your grandfather. He's awake!"

Declan took his thumb off the hose's nozzle, shutting off the spray. He'd much rather stay at the nursery than return to the hospital, but one look at his mom's anxious face helped him make his decision. "Let me talk to Mr. Neal."

"I already did," Gloria said. "Hurry! We don't know how much time we have."

We. Was that like a collective we, or did it mean she had someone—and by someone, he meant his stepfather—with her? He rolled up the hose as quickly as he could while his mom fluttered with impatience beside him.

"I'll be back as soon as I can," he called to Mr. Neal on his way out the door. His steps slowed when he caught

sight of Godwin's mammoth Mercedes idling in the nearly empty gravel parking lot.

Godwin glared at him through the darkly tinted windows.

Declan looked down and realized he was still wearing the bright yellow Neal's Nursery apron. He also had water and mud splattered on his jeans and dirt clung to his fingernails. He took off the apron and used it to wipe off his hands before he climbed into Godwin's car. Wadding it into a ball, he dropped it on the floor beside his muddy sneakers.

"I wish we had something more appropriate for you to wear," Gloria said.

"Do you want to swing by the house?" Godwin asked.

"No, no," Gloria said, casting Declan a worried glance over her shoulder. "He'll have to do."

He'll have to do? Do what? His mom was being ridiculous. She hated her dad. For nearly eighteen years, she'd had nothing to do with him, nothing to say to him, and now that the old man was dying, now that she had something to gain and something to lose, she wanted to play nice. It rankled him.

"My clothes are completely appropriate for working, which was my plan," Declan said, slouching lower into the back seat.

"There's work and then there's dirty work," Godwin said, looking at him through the rearview mirror. "You have to decide whether or not to get your hands dirty."

What does that even mean? Declan wondered. Was Godwin making a metaphor for life? Declan wasn't ashamed of working at the nursery. He liked it. Sure, Mr. Neal was sort of goofy, but he was also kind. Just that morning he'd been singing to the rhododendrons because he knew that old Mrs. Harper would be picking them up and transplanting them into her flower bed. He worried any time the plants left for a new home.

"I'm going to go to medical school," Declan said. "Medicine can be extremely messy. Do you have a problem with that?"

"Of course not." Gloria blew out a breath and scowled at Godwin.

Godwin used the rearview mirror to shoot Declan a look that said, *I have a problem with you.* At least that's what Declan thought it said, because just like he didn't speak plant or crow, he also didn't really get Godwin. And he didn't see how his mother could.

They rode to the hospital in an icy silence. Declan's hands grew cold and he tucked them under his arms to keep them warm. He refused to ask Godwin for anything—even a request for turning up the heat was more than his pride would allow.

They crossed over the Mercy Island Bridge and broached the hill leading to Queen Anne General, making Declan think of the first time he had met Lizbet. He smiled, in spite of himself, remembering how she'd thought she

needed a veteran or a Presbyterian to help find her mom. He had thought she was so strange... and he still did. Sort of.

"You need to look sad!" Gloria told him after she caught his eye in the mirror attached to her window shade. "It's bad enough you're dressed like a hillbilly!"

Declan's smile faded. A dark cloud hovered over the Queen Anne skyline... and his mood.

Weeks slid by. The police made little to no headway on the investigation, and if it wasn't for Elizabeth's pestering, Lizbet suspected they would have dropped it altogether. Lizbet settled into the ranch's quiet rhythm. She woke with the sun, helped Elizabeth feed the animals and puttered in the garden until Matías or Maria showed up to help her with her online classes. But one morning while Lizbet and Elizabeth were spreading feed for the chickens, visitors interrupted their newly established routine.

When Josie and a tall dark man with a widow's peak slid out of a large black Mercedes, Elizabeth softly swore, wiped her hands on her apron, and patted her silver curls into place.

Lizbet watched from the chicken pen while Elizabeth went to greet their guests. Something about the man pricked Lizbet's memory. Then she remembered him from the hospital. He'd asked her if she was a P.D. James fan. She

wondered how he knew Josie and why he was coming to visit Elizabeth.

They chatted with her grandmother for a few minutes, but they were too far away for Lizbet to hear their conversation above the chickens' jabbering. Minutes later, Elizabeth returned, looking perplexed and unhappy.

Lizbet waited for her grandmother to comment on the visitors. When Elizabeth returned to spreading the chicken feed with tight lips and a scowl etched between her eyebrows and Josie and the man walked across the fields, Lizbet decided not to pry, even though she really wanted to ask why both of them would chose to walk through a horse pasture wearing business attire.

"They're going to ruin their shoes," Elizabeth said with a smirk.

"Josie will snag her tights," Lizbet added.

"That's not all she's trying to snag," Elizabeth said. "I don't trust that Gaylord Godwin."

"Josie seems to. Who is he?"

"He's a local businessman and land developer. Josie has less animal instinct than the chickens. She wouldn't recognize a wolf in sheep's wool if he came up and blew her house down."

Elizabeth's expression and mood grew darker the longer Josie stayed. When Matías's beat-up truck pulled down the drive, Lizbet wiped her hands on her skirt, and left to start her studies.

Elizabeth just nodded as Lizbet headed for the house, Matías, and the sanctity of the computer.

Lizbet met Matías at the back porch.

"Who's here?" Matías asked, his eyes following the couple rounding the barn.

"Josie—she's my aunt—and some man."

"What are they doing? I mean, they don't look like they're here to ride horses or pick cherries."

Lizbet bumped him with her shoulder. "I'm sure Josie doesn't need an excuse to visit her mom."

Matías's lips twitched as he pulled open the back door and held it open for her. "What makes you so sure?"

She passed underneath his arm through the doorway and stopped in the mudroom to remove her dirty shoes. "I don't need a reason to visit my mom, other than I want to."

"Yeah, but you're you." Matías smiled down at her.

She didn't know what that meant, so she let it go.

"Want to start with calculus?" Matías asked, taking a chair beside her desk.

"No one ever wants to start with calculus," Lizbet muttered.

"Wrong. No one ever wants to start with bio," Matías said.

She just shook her head. He liked math and she loved biology—it was like they each spoke a different language... especially when they worked on her Spanish. Matías was fluent since his father was Hispanic. His mother was Native American. His family's dark coloring made Lizbet

feel like she belonged in a way she'd never felt with Elizabeth, Josie, or even her own pale mother.

Lizbet pulled up Lincoln Academy's website and resigned herself to calculus, even though she didn't know what possible use it could ever be. "What do you want to do, Matías? Will you stay on your dad's farm?"

"Only if he'll let me modernize it. We could do so much more, be so much more if he'd move out of the Stone Age."

"So you do want to stay?"

He cocked his head. "Yeah, but I want to study business and marketing. My dad has an okay thing going now, but the market for farm fresh produce is exploding and we're just scratching the surface."

"Like the chickens." Lizbet smiled.

"Exactly," Matías said. "How about you?"

"I don't know. I didn't look beyond the island because I didn't want to hurt my mom, but now... I don't think I could go back to the way things were, even when she gets better." *If she gets better.*

"So, if you could do anything, be anything," Matías pressed.

"I'd really like to travel."

"That's a far cry from hiding out on an island."

"It is, isn't it?"

"We better work on your Spanish."

They fell into a comfortable silence as they studied. Hours later, a rattling on the window interrupted them. Tennyson stood on the sill, his back arched.

"Someone wants in?" Matías asked.

Lizbet pushed away from the desk, stretched, and went outside to get her cat.

"Those people are up to no good," Tennyson said as soon as Lizbet pulled him off the ledge and into her arms.

"What do you mean?" Lizbet asked, after she rounded a corner and was sure Matías couldn't hear or see her.

"They plan on turning the ranch into a resort—they called it a dude ranch."

"A resort? Elizabeth won't let them do that."

"That's their plan," Tennyson said. *"The female thinks Elizabeth shouldn't be living out her by herself. She thinks it's dangerous. She said, and I quote, 'My mother is getting stranger and stranger every day.'"*

"But it's Elizabeth's ranch. She should be able to live here no matter what."

"I'm just passing on what I heard." Tennyson snuggled into her.

"Where does Josie think Elizabeth should live?"

Tennyson flicked his tail in response while Lizbet wondered what it would mean if Elizabeth did move off the ranch. Would she move in with Josie? Surely Josie wouldn't want that, right? And where would Lizbet stay? Maybe they would continue to let her stay on the ranch. She gazed over the pasture at the horses. They were the most visible of the animals, but Lizbet knew a whole society lived in the tall grass. There were mice, chipmunks, moles, foxes, and

too many insects to count. She and Elizabeth wouldn't be the only ones displaced.

Still cradling Tennyson, Lizbet went inside and sat down at the desk. She tried to focus on her studies, but her mind was racing.

"So, do you want to come?"

A beat too late, she realized that Matías had been talking to her.

"Of course," she said brightly, trying to hide the fact that she had no idea what she'd just agreed to.

"You don't understand," Lizbet said to Maria. "It's not that I don't want to go to your graduation party. It's that I don't have anything to wear. And—" She waved her hand over her face, indicating that she didn't have any makeup. "I have money," she said. "Although I really shouldn't. If Elizabeth would only charge me for food and rent, I wouldn't feel so indebted."

Maria wrapped her arm around Lizbet's shoulder. "I know Elizabeth loves having you here."

"How much is she paying you and Matías for tutoring me?"

Maria's eyes shifted away. "I can't tell you, but—"

"No buts!" Lizbet stood and flounced over to her closet. "I hate feeling like a freeloader!" She rifled through the few hanging dresses, skirts, and blouses she had brought with her.

"Believe me, you are not a freeloader! Running a farm is a lot of work, and you're doing more than your fair share! According to my dad, Elizabeth is slowing down. He said she wouldn't be able to stay here if it wasn't for you."

Lizbet blinked back fast hot tears. She hadn't yet told anyone what Tennyson had overheard about Josie thinking her mom shouldn't stay at the ranch, but she knew that moving would kill Elizabeth. "It's not enough. I should do more."

"Look, I have some old clothes I've outgrown. You could have them."

"And then I'll just be indebted to you!"

"Don't think of it like that!" Maria said. "Think of it as saving me a trip to the consignment shop."

"Consignment shop?" An idea clicked in Lizbet's mind. Elizabeth had rooms and closets, not to mention a basement and attic, full of stuff. Maybe Lizbet could sell a few things to help pay her way. And maybe while she was at the consignment shop, she could find a few new—to her—outfits.

Maria squealed when Lizbet shared her idea. Together they ran to find Elizabeth to see what she thought.

Declan and Beetle stood at the corner of East Fifth and McLeod directly in front of Cat's Consignment Shop.

People and cars passed by, but he only had eyes for the girls he could see through the large window. Lizbet. But instead of her typical hippie-looking skirt, she wore a pair of tight-fitting jeans, red cowboy boots, and a white blouse. She looked ridiculous. And yet... not.

She and the girl with her, another brunette, but taller and curvier, were trying on hats and laughing at their reflections in the mirror. Declan stepped to the side so they wouldn't catch him spying on them.

How did Lizbet always manage to spin him off balance? She wasn't his type.

"Declan!"

He turned to face Nicole. She hurried his way, her blond hair blowing around her face. He had to remind himself that Nicole was exactly his type, and now that they were both going to Duke there was nothing to stop them from...

From what? He had four years of undergrad, four years of medical school, and at least four years of a residency program ahead of him. And how was he going to pay for it all? He didn't have the time or money to date.

"Hey." Even to himself, he sounded flat. When Nicole's smile drooped, he tried to inject some enthusiasm into his voice. "How are you?"

How are you? Lame. But what should he have said?

"Good," she answered, her smile brightening. "Beetle, right?" She reached down and rubbed the dog between the ears. "How are you?" she asked the dog. "Does Declan treat you well?"

"He belongs to a neighbor. She broke her hip."

Nicole smiled up at him. "And you're helping her out? Wow, that's so good of you. You're one of the kindest people I know."

His smile felt false. He needed to tell her that he wasn't walking the dog to score brownie points—he did it for money. He opened his mouth to say the words, but nothing came out. He'd much rather be considered kind than poor.

The consignment store door swung open and Lizbet and the other brunette came out carrying multiple shopping bags. Lizbet had ditched the cowboy hat, but she was still wearing the red boots.

"Declan!" she said. "Hey there," she said to Nicole. "You're the girl who threw that party, right?"

"Right," Nicole said with a nod. "Hey, Maria."

Maria and Nicole hugged while Declan, Beetle, and Lizbet stood watching.

"Are you coming tonight?" Maria asked Nicole.

"Of course," Nicole said. "Wouldn't miss it. It's like a preview of my graduation party—but with better food."

"If you want my mom's empanada recipe, just ask," Maria said.

"It wouldn't be the same," Nicole said.

Declan wanted to ask where they were going, but he didn't want to sound like he was begging for an invite.

Nicole elbowed him. "Are you coming? You should."

"I wasn't invited," Declan said.

"You are now," Maria told him.

"Are you sure?" Declan asked. "I don't want there to be a shortage of empanadas." A shortage of empanadas? Really? Why was it so awkward to be around Nicole and Lizbet? He had a hard time with just Nicole, but somehow having Lizbet around made it a zillion times worse.

"Sure," Maria said.

Nicole blinked at him. "Pick me up around eight?"

"Um, okay," Declan said, hyper-aware of Lizbet's gaze on his face.

Nicole leaned in to kiss his cheek. "Great! Okay, see you."

"I guess we'll see you tonight," Maria said to Declan after Nicole swung away.

"Where am I going?" Declan asked. He knew he should be elated, but he felt flat and lifeless inside.

Maria laughed and told him her address.

"Just a minute, let me put it in my phone."

"I'll do it for you," Maria said, taking it from him.

Declan met Lizbet's gaze. He looked away first, feeling guilty, but he didn't know why.

After he thanked Maria, said goodbye, and pulled Beetle toward the park, he heard Lizbet say to Maria, "I thought she had a boyfriend."

"So did I," Maria said.

That was what Declan had thought, too.

Music thrummed through the kitchen. Lizbet, who was totally unfamiliar with any sort of ethnic food, was fascinated with Mrs. Hernandez and the way her fingers flew over the empanadas. She tried to help, but it took her five times as long to make one misshapen doughy ball. She wanted to try taquitos because they looked a lot easier, but Mrs. Hernandez shooed her out of the kitchen and into the thick of the party.

It wasn't that Lizbet didn't want to dance, or watch others dance, or watch Nicole drape herself over Declan, it was just that she wasn't used to so many people gathered in one place.

The dying sun cast shadows over the crowd. She and Maria had spent the afternoon hanging twinkly lights in the trees lining the Hernandez's' backyard. Beyond the trees and split-rail fence lay long stretches of pasture. Lizbet wondered how Maria and Matías's family would feel about a hotel resort moving in next door. She felt guilty for not telling them, but what could she say? *My cat told me my aunt wants to turn this place into a ritzy dude ranch?* She'd have to find some way to spill the news to both the Hernandez's and her grandmother.

Or she'd have to find a way to stop her aunt. The idea hit her so hard she choked on her drink. Horchata, she reminded herself. The drink's name sounded like it belonged to Nicole, or her aunt. Not nice, she scolded herself.

She had no reason to call Nicole a horchata. She seemed like a nice person. So what if she pressed herself up against Declan when they danced? Lots of girls were doing that. Maybe she could ask Matías to turn off the slow songs. She'd helped him pick out the night's soundtrack, so she really only had herself to blame.

"Want to dance?" Matías's breath blew across the back of her neck, making her feel ticklish and squirmy.

"Sure, Although, I have to warn you, I'm not very good."

Matías's face crinkled in a smile. "You don't have to do anything but put your arms around my waist and sway."

He was right, it didn't look hard. Some of the couples were hardly moving. Still. "Can we stay near the edge, out of the light?" Away from Declan and Nicole?

He shrugged, took her hand, and pulled her into his arms. He felt solid and comfortable. "No one's going to be watching your dancing," he said.

"I know. Especially now that we're in the darkest corner."

"Doesn't matter. What I meant was, they'll be so busy looking at your face, they won't be watching your feet."

That was a compliment. She wasn't sure what to do with it. One quick glance at Matías's face told her that she was more than a calculus pupil to him. Maybe more than a friend. She wasn't sure what to do with that, either. She rummaged in her head for something to say.

"Matías, if you knew or suspected something—something big, something that could impact a lot of people, and not

in a good way— would you find a way to tell them, even if you didn't know for sure..." Okay, so maybe this wasn't the best time to tell him, or anyone, but it did catch his interest.

"Of course. What do you know?"

"Remember, I don't know for sure. It's just something I thought I overheard."

"What is it already?"

She told him about her aunt's plans.

He pulled away from her as if she'd slapped him. "What do you think about this?"

"I think it's terrible! Mostly for Elizabeth. I know she doesn't want to trade her home for a dude ranch."

"I have to tell my dad," Matías said, letting her go and turning away.

"Remember... nothing's sure," she called after him, feeling sick. "I could be mistaken." She shouldn't have told him. She felt like she'd just poured a gallon of lighter fluid on spark and watched it turn into a blaze. What had she been thinking? Now she'd upset not only Matías, but potentially his father as well. And she only had the word of her cat to go on.

From Declan's Research
Traditional worship practices are often
a part of tribal gatherings with dance,
rhythm, songs and trance.

Chapter Ten

"What was that about?"

She hadn't noticed Declan coming up behind her. His voice sent a tremor down her spine. She shook her head, feeling dizzy with remorse. "I'm spreading rumors."

"Really? Interesting. I want to hear."

Lizbet looked around for Nicole. She'd been plastered to Declan all night. What had he used to pry himself loose?

"Want to dance?" he asked.

"Not really," she admitted. "I don't know how, and I'm terrible at it." But dancing wasn't the only thing she was terrible at. She felt awkward and out of place in all social situations. Maybe the island had been the right place for her.

He laughed. "I don't believe you."

"It's true... I don't think I can do this." She waved at the party.

"Define this," Declan said, concern touching his voice.

"I'm not good with people. I think I probably upset Matías, and I didn't mean to..."

"He'll get over it." Declan' voice was firm. "Want to go for a walk?"

She breathed out a long sigh. "I would love that."

He placed his hand on her arm and guided her through a break in the trees. Moments later, they were in the field. The moon skimmed the top of the hills, and the music, while still audible, dropped to a soft background noise.

"I'm not used to so many people," she admitted.

"I'm used to people, but I don't always love them," Declan said.

"But what about Nicole? Aren't you with her?"

"I picked her up, yes."

"Don't you think she'll miss you?"

He glanced over his shoulder. "Right now, she's too busy toying with Jason. I doubt she'll notice I'm gone."

"That's her old boyfriend, right?"

"Old, new, current—really, it's hard to say."

"No, it's not. It might be hard for you to guess, but for her, all she has to do is say whichever it is."

He chuckled softly. "True, but right now, she's keeping everyone guessing." He shook his head. "Going anywhere with her is a mistake."

"I'm sorry." Lizbet bit her lip and laced her fingers through his. She thought he might pull away, but he didn't.

"What for? You didn't make me drive to her house and pick her up."

She smiled. "No, I wouldn't have done that."

He pulled her further from the party. The tall grass slapped against her new boots and jeans, but she didn't care.

"You're not like other girls."

"I know. You've told me that before."

He laughed.

"For one thing, I can't dance."

"You were doing fine with Matías."

"You were watching?"

He nodded.

She sighed. "I feel like a giraffe out there—not really sure what to do with my arms and legs."

"It's easy, and I promise you, you are the least giraffe-looking girl here."

"You're sweet."

"Not really. I'm about to ditch my date."

Lizbet cast a quick glance at the trees separating them from the party. It was hard to know what Nicole was thinking or doing, but Lizbet guessed she wasn't really too concerned about Declan. She, herself, on the other hand was having a hard time being concerned about anyone else.

"Want to dance?" Declan asked.

"What? Here?"

"Why not?" He put his hands on her waist and pulled her close. "This is a perfect place to practice."

The music turned from a slow jazzy number to something with a faster pulse. Lizbet knew that in order to keep time with the music they needed to do more than shuffle their feet in a long embrace, but she leaned her head against Declan's chest, listened to the steady beat of his heart, and matched her movements to his.

He cupped her face. His eyes held a question and she knew her gaze couldn't answer him. She didn't know what they were doing. Nothing like this had ever happened to her before. When he kissed her, she forgot about questions or answers. She wasn't thinking about Nicole, Matías, Maria, or any of the others at the party through the trees. All her senses drowned in his kiss. She clung to his shoulders, afraid that she might lose track of herself as well. Of all the things that had turned her life upside down in the past few weeks, this was maybe the most earth-quaking, and yet, the best.

By far.

From Declan's Research
"Be praised, my Lord, through our sister
Mother Earth, who feeds us and rules us,
and produces various fruits with
colored flowers and herbs."
—Francis of Assisi

Chapter Eleven

Lizbet woke late the next morning. The sun had risen hours before, meaning the animals would be snorting and wanting their breakfast. She bounced from the bed, threw on a pair of overalls and a T-shirt, tied her hair up in a bandana, and padded down the stairs. About halfway to the mudroom, she knew they had a visitor.

Lizbet's Spanish had barely moved out of the taco and burrito phase, but she could tell from Perez's raised, tense tone that he was unhappy. Lizbet froze as her mind raced. Of course Matías had gone to his father with the news of the dude ranch. She had known that would happen. How could she explain this to Elizabeth? Her shoulders sagged as she walked into the living room, debating how she could fix the mess she'd made.

Wearing jeans, a denim shirt, and a pair of boots, Perez stood near the fireplace wringing a baseball cap in his hands. As she gazed into his weather-beaten face, Lizbet tried to imagine how a neighboring dude ranch would impact him. She knew that Elizabeth and Perez shared pastures.

Elizabeth folded her arms and faced her granddaughter. "Perez tells me that my daughter plans on turning my ranch into a resort and that this information came from you." Anger and resentment echoed through Elizabeth's words, but Lizbet knew the anger wasn't necessarily completely directed at her. "Do you care to share with me how you came to this conclusion?"

"I overheard them talking when they came by," Lizbet said. "Maybe they had been talking about another ranch. I wasn't sure. I didn't want to say anything to you in case I was mistaken."

Elizabeth raised her eyebrow. "Were you spying on them?"

"No!" Lizbet gulped. "But sometimes you hear and see things you don't want to hear or see."

"Humph. In some cases, and in ones such as this, I prefer spying," Elizabeth said, turning from Lizbet to Perez. "There is nothing to be done but to confront my Josie."

"Wait," Lizbet said, holding up her hands. "Maybe we should wait until we know for sure."

"And how can we do that?" Elizabeth balled her fists and planted them on her hips.

"I just think that..." Lizbet swallowed, intimidated by Elizabeth's let's-fight glare. She cleared her throat and started again. "Why stir up problems without cause? If it's not your ranch they wish to convert and they were just making comparisons—"

"Do you think that's the case?" Elizabeth arched an eyebrow.

"No, but... I really think we should give Josie the benefit of the doubt."

Elizabeth and Perez exchanged glances and a string of incomprehensible words. When their conversation paused, Lizbet quickly added, "If they are planning on converting your ranch and you don't want them to, don't you think we should put together a counterattack? I'm sure Josie will have compiled a compelling reason why she thinks you should do this."

Elizabeth raked her fingers through her hair, letting Lizbet know that her grandmother was not the sit, wait, and strategize sort. She was obviously the kick-butt and ask questions later kind. No wonder she and bossy Josie didn't get along.

"And how do you suggest we find out Josie's plans?"

"I don't know..." Lizbet's mind grabbed at fleeting ideas, but none of them were good enough to hold on to. Sure, she could send a few furry animals into Josie's apartment or office, but they couldn't read so unless they overheard something, they'd be useless spies. "Let me do some reading on dude ranches. Then we'll invite her to

lunch and just talk to her. We can ask about her plans in general. If she brings up the dude ranch, hopefully we'll have some persuasive reasons why this won't work."

Elizabeth still scowled, but she didn't look quite so huffy. "I'll think about it, but I have to warn you, once Josie gets an idea in her head, you need a crowbar to wedge it out." She jabbed her finger at Lizbet's chest. "I'm calling and scheduling a lunch right now!" She made this sound like a threat.

Lizbet swallowed. "I'll do some research as soon as I'm done with the morning chores."

But the bulk of her research was spent with the animals. The chickens knew nothing about Josie's plans. The goats were too busy butting each other in the head to carry on any sort of conversation, but the horses were a wealth of information, mostly because none of them wanted to be turned into horses for hire.

"It's flagrant prostitution!" Angel, the appaloosa whinnied.

Trotter, an Arabian, tossed his head in agreement, sending his silky mane to cover his eyes. *"We can't be expected to trot and tote around any Joe or Jane. All these city-slicker cowboy wannabes, they're all kick and slap and no sugar cubes."*

"But you know for sure they were talking about this ranch and not some other, maybe even hypothetical, ranch?" Lizbet asked.

"There's more than this ranch?" Angel neighed, sounding skeptical.

"No." Trotter shook his mane again, this time uncovering his large black eyes. *"This pasture is all there is. I've traveled enough to know that beyond this pasture there is endless forest. We are the only horses, and Elizabeth's ranch is all there is. That's why so many will come for the pleasure of riding on our backs."*

"It's true, you are the only horses in Elizabeth's ranch, but..." Lizbet began.

"Then this conversion, this pollution, destroys our world as we know it!" Angel's voice rang with panic.

"There's more to this world than Elizabeth's ranch," Lizbet assured the animals.

"This pasture is our world!" Trotter stomped his hooves to emphasize his words.

Angel's eyes widened with fear.

"Okay, stay calm," Lizbet said, trying to sound soothing. "I'll see what—if anything—I can do."

But after a few hours at her computer, she came to the sad realization that Elizabeth's ranch probably would make a wonderful resort. It was close enough to Queen Anne to be convenient, but far enough away to ensure privacy and a rural setting. The house already had six bedrooms and the attic could easily be converted to allow for a few more—especially if they added on over the garage. The property had at least seven outbuildings, not including the garage, and they could also be converted into guest rooms.

No.

She couldn't think this way. The property belonged to Elizabeth and if she didn't want a dude ranch she shouldn't be wrangled into one. Lizbet had to prove why a dude ranch was a bad idea.

But wait. Why? The property belonged to Elizabeth. That should be the end of the argument. But knowing Josie, it probably wouldn't be. So how could Lizbet change Josie's mind? A kernel of an idea took shape.

Elizabeth banged into the kitchen and slammed her canning pot onto the table. "We're going to meet Josie for lunch tomorrow at her office." She lined up a bunch of carrots on the cutting board and selected a long sharp butcher knife. "She doesn't have time to meet us today." Elizabeth began to whack at the carrots, whittling them down into sticks with such force that Lizbet nearly felt sorry for them.

"Tomorrow?" Perfect, Lizbet thought. That would be enough time.

Long after Elizabeth had gone to bed, Lizbet crawled from her own. Pulling on her overalls and a soft hoodie, she padded from her room, down the stairs, and into the kitchen where she stole a block of cheddar cheese from the refrigerator. After slipping on her boots in the mudroom, she cracked open the back door and silently stole across the yard, heading for the barn.

A thick mist hung in the air, shrouding the moon. The animals' warm breath rose in the sky. Lizbet shivered, knowing what she was about to ask was dangerous, even life-threatening.

It took a few minutes for her eyes to adjust to the barn's gloomy interior. She inhaled deeply, sucking in the animal smells mingled with hay and leather. While the horses and goats slept, Lizbet knew an entire population of creatures scurried inside the walls, under the floor, and across the barn beams. These were the animals she needed to speak to.

Squatting, she took the cheese from the pocket of her hoodie and began to crumble it between her fingers. She smiled when she noticed a sudden stillness. She'd gotten the attention of the rodents.

"Friends," she spoke into the darkness, "I need your help."

No one answered, but she imagined dozens if not hundreds of twitching noses and trembling whiskers in the semi-darkness.

"As you may have heard, there are plans to convert our ranch into a resort. As I'm sure you are aware, this will be life-altering and even life-threatening for most of you. You depend on the pastures surrounding the ranch in some way. For many of you, it's your home, a food source, and a place of peace and security. Take away the pastures, and for most of you, your quality of life will skid downhill."

Lizbet tossed chunks of cheese into the dark. Claw sounds skittered across the floor. "I know you have no

reason to trust me, but frankly, we are in this together. I don't want Elizabeth to lose her home any more than you want to lose yours."

A few bright eyes emerged from the darkness.

"I have a plan. It will be dangerous."

A large rat scuttled in front of her. He sat back on his haunches and snaked his tail in front of him. *"I'm Raphael, the rat king. I would like to hear your proposal."*

"I can't promise it will work," Lizbet said just before launching into her plan and setting a large burlap sack on the floor in front of her.

A few minutes later, Lizbet cinched the burlap bag closed and hefted it over her shoulder as she climbed onto Trotter's back. "I'm sorry about the close quarters," she said to the mice and rats scrambling inside the bag. "This will be easier for everyone if you try and hold still."

"How far is the journey, miss?" Trotter asked.

"According to the GPS, nine miles," Lizbet told him. "But it will be faster for us because we can cut through fields and woods."

"Nine miles. But I've never been nine miles!"

Lizbet patted his neck and tightened her grip the reins. "It's like I told you, there's a great big world out there." She realized then as she moved through the dark night,

that she and Trotter had a lot in common. There was a time where Blackstone Island had been her whole world. She hadn't been able to see beyond it, because that was all she knew, just like Trotter couldn't see beyond the ranch.

While the rats and mice skittered inside the jostling sack, Lizbet tried to enjoy the midnight ride. Her mother's stories haunted her. Over and over, she reminded herself that in the weeks since she'd left the island, nothing horrible had happened to her. She hadn't bumped into one cruel person, or been confronted by evil. Sure, she knew evil existed. Occasionally, she watched the news with Elizabeth and that often confirmed her mom's worst nightmares, but Lizbet had yet to meet a gun-toting lunatic.

Although, maybe, if she was to meet one now, this would be the very worst time. Being alone on a dark night was a very bad idea.

She told herself she was safe on Trotter's back. And someone might have a gun, but she had a bag of rodents. The rats and mice might not be as scary as a firearm, but a rodent army could still be a very valuable and effective weapon. She'd just have to take her chances.

It surprised her that Josie lived only nine miles away in East End and not in Queen Anne itself. She would have thought Josie would choose to live in a swanky downtown apartment close to her work. But maybe Josie wasn't as different from her mom and sister as she pretended to be.

Because they were able to take shortcuts through trails and woods, it didn't take nearly as long as Lizbet had thought it would to reach the gates of Josie's condo complex.

Trotter pranced in front of gates. *"Should I try to jump? I've never jumped a fence before."*

"No," Lizbet said, resigning herself to climbing over the gates. She climbed off Trotter, and tried to shift the bag of rodent as gently as she could. Her legs felt wobbly after the long ride. She set the bag down on the ground, and found a tree where she could tie Trotter.

"If anyone tries to steal you, kick them," Lizbet instructed the horse. "You don't need to be kind."

Trotter blew out a friendly breath, nickered, and shook his head at her as Lizbet headed for the large wrought-iron gates. To her amazement, they swung open.

She turned just as a car rolled down the drive. She dove into the bushes, but not before she locked eyes with Declan sitting behind the wheel of an ancient Honda.

Lizbet crouched in the bushes, prepared to run if Declan reappeared. She waited, and as she did, time crawled to a stop. He had to have seen her. Was he looking for her? Or did he think she made a habit of prowling around condo complexes in the middle of the night? At least he didn't know about the bag of rodents. Yet.

After several minutes crawled by on turtle speed, she crept from her hiding place, hoisted the bag over her shoulder and followed the GPS' instructions to her aunt's

condo. She took note of the dark windows. What if Josie wasn't home?

Lizbet tried the front door and the back patio door, but both were locked. Her gaze traveled up to an open second-story window. "Here we go," she whispered to the rodents. "Be safe," she told them as she released the cinch. "This is a noble thing you're doing. Remember, cause as much havoc as you can and as soon as things get dangerous, head for the woods. I'll leave the bag here waiting for you."

The rodents scurried out, followed her pointing finger, and easily scaled the wall to the window.

Lizbet retreated to the woods with her bag to wait and listen. It didn't take long. Josie's light switched on and the screaming started. Lizbet wanted to cheer. Everything about her plan was going perfectly... until she spotted Declan standing in the parking lot, looking directly at her.

Chapter Twelve

Lizbet thought about moving deeper into the woods, but then Declan could stumble upon the rodents when they retreated. Knowing she had a responsibility to protect the critters, she took a deep breath, and went to face Declan and his questions. She found him in the parking lot beside his car.

"What are you doing?" he asked.

"My aunt lives here," she replied.

"Your aunt? You don't like your aunt."

"She's still my mother's sister. And besides, that's why I'm outside her condo instead of inside." She tucked her hands into her pockets, afraid he'd notice how dirty they were. "What are you doing?"

"I live here."

"You do? But I've been to your house..."

He pointed his chin at a neighboring condo. "I live with my dad."

Josie's screams rang through the air. Several lights flashed on.

"I wonder what's going on," Declan said.

"My aunt is watching a slasher movie," Josie said.

"That's coming from your aunt's condo?"

"She's watching *The Zombie Wars*."

He cocked his head at her. "I wouldn't have pegged you as a zombie chick."

"I'm not. That's one of the reasons I'm out here." She laughed, but hated how nervous she sounded. She turned so that Declan had to have his back to Josie's window to look at her. A few rodents had gathered on the windowsill and they watched her with their beady eyes. In the distance, Trotter nickered.

"Did you see that someone tied a horse up to the fence?"

"What? Really?" She hated lying to him.

"Weird, right?" Declan asked.

"So weird..." *Weirder than you know.*

He glanced at his phone. "I better go inside, my dad's worried about me."

Lizbet watched the rodents scurry down the wall. They formed a straight line like soldiers on parade. If Declan turned around now, he'd be sure to see them. She had to

stall. Scrambling for something to say, she came up with, "That must be nice."

"What?"

"Your dad worries about you."

The rodents scampered across the patio while upstairs Josie screamed, "Out! Out!"

Lizbet pulled her hoodie over her head, just in case Josie happened to look out the window. "You have your dad, your mom, even a stepfather... probably even cousins. I only have my mom."

"You have Elizabeth and your aunt."

"You're right." She smiled at him.

"He says he'll always worry about me."

"How very worrisome."

"Mmm." Declan stepped closer, as if to kiss her.

She lifted her face to his, but because she had one eye trained on the rodents trooping down the condo wall, she couldn't enjoy herself the way she wanted to. Hopefully, there would be many more kisses in the future.

He squeezed her hand. "You should go inside, too."

"I will, as soon as the movie's over."

Declan looked at his phone. "When will that be?"

"Soon," Lizbet said, watching the trickling line of rodents. "I'm okay out here, really."

He still looked doubtful, so she walked with him to his door.

"Do you want to come in?" he asked.

"And give your dad something to really worry about?"

He waggled his eyebrows. "Yeah."

She laughed. "No." And placed her hand on his chest to push him against his front door.

"Declan?"

A man poked his head out the window. Lizbet froze as she gazed into the eyes of John Lamb.

"I'll be right in, Dad," Declan said.

Dad.

"Who's your friend?" he asked. Lizbet recognized his voice from a hundred visits to her mom.

"Lizbet Westmoor, Elizabeth Westmoor's granddaughter."

John Lamb's widened in recognition. He knows, Lizbet thought.

"Josie's daughter?" Disbelief touched his voice.

Maybe he doesn't know, Lizbet thought.

"Her aunt is watching a zombie movie," Declan explained, "and she's hiding out here."

"That's wise." John Lamb's expression crinkled with kindness and questions.

Somehow, Lizbet stumbled through introductions, and answered questions about her mom, grandmother, and aunt. "I have to go," she said, her heart hammering. She tore away, and ducked around the corner of the closest building. When she was sure Declan and John were out of sight, she ran for the woods.

"Everyone here and accounted for?" she whispered.

The rodents had refilled the bag. *"Yes,"* came a hundred muffled replies.

"Good," Lizbet said. But as she along with Trotter and the rodents retraced their steps toward Elizabeth's ranch, Lizbet had to admit that nothing was good, at all. Because if John Lamb was her dad, as she believed, that made Declan her brother. With a heavy heart, she came to grips with the fact that there wouldn't be future kisses with Declan.

Of course maybe John wasn't her father—but then who was? She knew for certain that John and her mother were lovers. Lizbet couldn't keep on kissing Declan on the rare chance that they weren't siblings. A tiredness that had nothing to do with the late hour pressed against Lizbet's mind. She felt numb. Her earlier jubilation completely deflated, and she wondered with detachment what would become of her.

She hadn't realized how much she had come to like Declan until the possibility of him ever being more than a brotherly-sort of friend disappeared.

Lizbet convinced Elizabeth to put on a dress and a pair of heels for the lunch with Josie. Despite the fact that the black crinoline was snug, smelled of mothballs, and was horribly outdated, Elizabeth looked much better and more polished than Lizbet had ever seen her. It had

taken some coaxing to get Elizabeth in the "Sunday best" clothes, and even more for her to allow Lizbet free rein on her hair, but now that they were both "spit polished and shined," as Elizabeth said, Lizbet was glad.

Lizbet didn't know if Josie had intentionally picked out an intimidating restaurant, or if she typically spent her lunch hours at cafes where the waiters only spoke French. She suspected that Josie wanted to send a clear message to her mother that when it came to finances, Josie knew best.

But whatever swagger Josie had hoped to swing, one look at her exhausted face told Lizbet that for today, at least, Josie had lost her mojo. And Lizbet knew she had the rats and mice to thank.

Swallowing a secret smile, she followed the garcon across the slate floor to the atrium. Flowers and exotic plants lined the walls. Vines hung from the beams of the glass ceiling. The sun-filled room was almost as heavenly as the odors wafting through air. Everything was beautiful, except for Josie's haggard expression.

Elizabeth settled into a wrought iron chair. The garcon whipped out her linen napkin and dropped it onto her lap. "Oh, thank you," she said with giggle. "It's not often I have handsome young men fawning over me!" She winked at the tall lean man with a drooping mustache, named Pierre.

"What's with you, mother?" Josie huffed as soon as Pierre was out of earshot.

"Why, what do you mean?" Elizabeth asked as she snagged a croissant from the silver breadbasket.

"You're—" Josie waved a hand in front of her mom.

"You're the one who's always telling me to stop dressing like a farmhand and spiffy up." Elizabeth tore into her roll and a puff of warm, fragrant air escaped. She smiled as if the croissant were singing her name.

Josie leaned forward and braced her elbows on the table. "You were flirting with the waiter."

"Oh, do you think? I thought he was flirting with me!" She looked over her shoulder, made eye contact with Pierre and waggled her fingers at him.

Josie slapped her mom's wrist. "Mother! Stop it!"

Lizbet quickly picked up her water goblet and took a sip to hide her smile.

"He's only being kind because he's hoping you'll leave him a tip!" Josie hissed.

Elizabeth's grin didn't fade. "Just because you're not looking your best, doesn't mean I need to play Dowdy-Dora."

Josie straightened her shoulders and pulled herself into a haughty position for a fleeting moment. Then she sagged, as if wilting, and rubbed a tired hand across her eyes. "You're right. I'm not at my best today," she admitted.

Elizabeth peered at her through suspicious eyes. Lizbet guessed that Elizabeth wasn't used to seeing her younger daughter in a vulnerable state.

"Last night my condo was completely overrun with vermin!" Josie spat out the last word.

Elizabeth looked shocked. "Did you call the manager?"

"Yes, but... he didn't believe me!"

"How could he not believe you?" Elizabeth set down her croissant. "Either you have a rodent infestation or you don't."

"He says we don't." She took a long sip of wine. "Last night the rodents were having a party in my room. Today, there's no sign of them."

"Did you talk to your neighbors?" Elizabeth prodded.

Josie nodded. "I'm the only one who saw them."

"Well!" Elizabeth huffed. "That just won't do! Do you want to come and stay at the ranch?"

Lizbet noted the indecision battling in Josie's expression. "Well..."

"You know, it's your home, too," Elizabeth said, smiling as if an idea light bulb had suddenly been illuminated over her head.

"I've been wanting to talk to you about the ranch," Josie said, but her voice had lost her typical enthusiasm and confidence.

Elizabeth batted her eyelashes. "What about the ranch?"

"Oh, never mind, maybe this isn't the best time, but I do think you should be open to..." Her voice faltered. "So you wouldn't mind if I came and stayed with you just until I can be sure the exterminator is successful?" Her tone turned steely. "I had to hire him myself, because the manager refused."

Josie fell quiet when Pierre returned with a tray of food. She waited until he was gone to continue. "They can't come

out until next week. Next week!" She pierced a piece of her crepe with her fork and shook it at her mother. "I can't stay there. I won't stay there!"

Elizabeth patted Josie's knee. "Of course not, darling. You know you always have a home on the ranch."

Josie sniffed, nibbled on her lunch, and tried to look brave while Elizabeth prattled on about the farm, her garden, and the horses who were expecting to foal.

Lizbet smiled as she ate her excellent lunch of quiche Lorraine. She knew everything had gone exactly as she had planned when Josie muttered, "This is not how I thought this lunch would go."

"What do you mean, sweetie?" Elizabeth asked. "It was a lovely lunch."

Josie sighed, looked defeated, and took a long swallow of wine.

From Declan's Research
"There is no fundamental difference between man and the higher animals in their mental faculties... The lower animals, like man, manifestly feel pleasure and pain, happiness, and misery."
—Charles Darwin

Chapter Thirteen

An hour or so later, Lizbet sat beside her comatose mother, held her hand, and willed her to wake. "I don't think I can do this anymore without you," she said.

Her mother didn't move. Her whispered breath was nearly inaudible, her posture completely relaxed. The only thing that let Lizbet know her mother was alive was the bedside monitor's beeping lights and steady hum. But Lizbet had to talk to someone.

"Elizabeth wants me to go to school, but even the community college is expensive. Matías and Maria have walked me through the forms for financial aid, but it's all so foreign." Anger simmered inside Lizbet, but she pushed it down. Her mother must have had her reasons for keeping them isolated on Blackstone Island. Being angry with her mom wouldn't help anyone.

"I just can't help wondering if Josie needs money. I mean, why else would she want to sell her mother's ranch?" Lizbet leaned her head against the cold, smooth wall. On the island, everyday had a purpose. They had to tend the garden, or they wouldn't eat. They had to gather wood, or they would be cold. Life had been simpler and yet, harder. And yes, there were still chores to do at Elizabeth's ranch, but Elizabeth seemed much more concerned with Lizbet's schooling, and Lizbet had yet to discover who she really was and what she wanted to do.

Declan wanted to go to medical school. If the community college was expensive, a medical school had to be much more. Her thoughts went back to her mother's use of medicinal herbs. Maybe she could study plants. Or animals. She loved them both and felt more like herself when she was around them.

She glanced at the tubes hooked up to her mom. What ran through them? What were they feeding her? Her mom looked even more pale than usual. Her lips nearly gray. Her eyelids were so thin that Lizbet could see blue veins running through them.

Something tickled in the back of her mind. She longed for her mom's herb garden. She could see the plant bundles drying on the rack hanging in the kitchen. She could smell them. But for them to be of any use at all, she needed her mom to taste and touch them. They were there and she was here. Her thoughts skipped to Leonard. He could

possibly take her, but since she and her mom were no longer living on Blackstone, he didn't have a need to go there. She knew how long his route took and she couldn't ask him to take her and lengthen it.

Declan... As much as she wanted to ask him, she couldn't. As long as she suspected they were siblings, she had to stay away from him. She didn't trust herself not to. She knew that brothers and sisters shouldn't feel the way she felt about him, but she'd spent so long being sure that John Lamb was her dad... And if he wasn't, then who was? Even she knew enough about biology to understand that, as far as she knew, there had only been one Immaculate Conception.

Elizabeth bustled into the room, looking both harried and relieved. "It's all settled. Josie will move in this evening after work."

"That's a good thing, right?" Lizbet asked.

Elizabeth blew out a sigh. "Yes. She didn't once mention turning my home into a dude ranch, and it seems unlikely that she'll wish to do so as long as she's living there. But I'm sure you've picked up on the fact that Josie and I don't have the best relationship. I love her dearly, but she hasn't been easy to live with since the day she was born. Her dad was much better with her than me..." Her voice softened. "I wish he were here now."

"What happened to him?" Lizbet asked.

Elizabeth settled into the chair on Rose's opposite side. "Losing Daugherty killed him. He loved both of his girls, but he doted on Daugherty. And then one day, she was just gone. He was frantic." She gazed at her daughter, her expression soft and full of longing. "I wish she knew how much we loved her, how desperately we searched for her."

"I wish I had known him," Lizbet said.

"He would have loved you," Elizabeth said, her eyes shining with unshed tears. "And you would have loved him, too."

Suddenly, Lizbet saw her mother as selfish and cruel, a thing she'd never imagined before.

"The years stretched on. I gave up, but Eddie never did. If anything, he became more frantic. It wore him out."

Could the strain of her mom's health wear out Elizabeth, too? Lizbet couldn't let that happen. She thought of the St. John's wort her mom had used to boost her energy, and all the other herbs.

"Elizabeth, I'd like to go back to the island. There are some things there that I need."

"Well, I'll call Declan again—"

"No!"

Elizabeth's eyebrows shot up.

"Not Declan!"

"Oh, now." Elizabeth's voice filled with disappointment. "I thought the two of you had hit it off."

"We did... I just... I can't." She stumbled for something to say, gave up, and just sighed.

Elizabeth seemed to understand. She stretched her arm across the bed and grabbed Lizbet's hand and gave it a squeeze. "You have enough to worry about without adding boy problems to the mix."

"Exactly," Lizbet breathed out, although, she knew that wasn't exactly it. Maybe she could find the herbs somewhere, somehow.

The next day after the morning chores had been completed and she'd finished her study session with Matías, Lizbet compiled list of herbs from her mother's favorite herbology book and begged a ride into town from Matías.

After depositing her at Neal's Nursery, Matías stuck his head out the window. "Are you sure you don't want me to swing by and pick you up?"

Lizbet shook her head and tried not to worry about the storm clouds gathering over the hills. "I really don't know how long I'll be, and I don't want to keep you waiting."

"It wouldn't be a problem." He gave her a sheepish smile. "I don't mind waiting for you."

"I'll see you tomorrow," she said, lacing her voice with what she hoped sounded like resolve, and turned her back on him. Her boots scrunched across the gravel parking lot, announcing her arrival to a small gathering of robins on a split-rail fence.

Lizbet glanced around, making sure they were alone before she addressed the birds. "Good afternoon. Are you familiar with this establishment?"

"Of course!" The robins chattered and cocked their heads. A few puffed out their red breasts and strutted around.

"Do you happen to know where to find the herbs?" Lizbet continued.

"They're this way," a deep voice answered.

Lizbet squealed in surprise and dropped her books when a middle-aged man stepped out from behind a honeysuckle covered lattice. Tall, gangly-thin, with hook-like nose, he looked like a friendly scarecrow.

"Did I scare you?" he asked.

Lizbet scrambled for an answer. She could say yes and admit to not seeing him, and he would wonder who she'd been speaking to. Or she could lie. Scooping up her books, she let her hair fall in front of her face, hoping to hide her confusion. Lizbet inspected her books for damage. They looked pretty much the same, despite their tumble on the gravel. They were old and beaten, and smelled of decay. When she did peek at the man, she caught his smile.

He leaned against his shovel. "I talk to myself all the time. Well, in reality, I'm talking to my plants, but according to my wife, it amounts to pretty much the same thing." His smile widened. "She said she won't be concerned until the plants start talking back."

"And have they?" Lizbet asked.

"I'll never tell," he said in a mock-serious tone.

"I don't blame you." Lizbet didn't have to hide her own seriousness.

He nudged his head to the left. "Come on, I'll show you my herbs."

She liked the way he said, my herbs, as if he had more than a commercial concern for them, as if he were invested in them emotionally as well.

"Is there something in particular you're looking for?"

Lizbet read off her list.

He lifted on eyebrow. "Sounds like you're making a healing poultice."

"How did you know?" Lizbet asked.

"I'm a botanist. Plants are my life." He turned and headed down a path lined with trellises of English ivy.

"So have you made a healing poultice before?" Lizbet followed him through the green tunnel.

He nodded.

"And did it work?" She wished she could see his face. As it was, all she could see was the broad set of his shoulders and the easy swing of his gait. This told her only that he considered himself an honest man.

"I've done several. Sometimes it worked. Once it didn't. But there's no saying whether it was the work of the herb, the passing of time, or the inevitable."

They emerged from the tunnel to a sunny patch of concrete where hundreds of potted herbs lined backless

wooden shelves. The sudden shift of light combined with the sharp, pungent odors of the plants made Lizbet feel faint for one brief but intense moment. She put her hand on her forehead, trying to gauge what was wrong with her.

"You okay?" the man asked, squinting as if trying to read her.

She nodded.

He took her elbow and steered her toward a wooden bench. They sat side by side. "Sometimes when I'm alone here, I feel a spiritual energy from the plants." He slid her a sideways glance. "Do you ever feel that way?"

She blinked at him. "I do."

He nodded, as if he had known how she would answer his question. "The plants are so uncomplicated. They need only the basics of water, sun, and soil to grow and don't ask for any more. They know that too much is too much. We humans can learn a lot from the plants."

"I love that," Lizbet answered, thinking back to the simplicity of the island. Her heart ached for her mom, reminding her of her mission. Climbing to her feet, she inspected the herbs. It didn't surprise her that all of Mr. Neal's plants were healthy and vibrant.

"Lizbet?"

She whirled, immediately recognizing Declan's voice. Sunlight kissed his hair. He wore the Neal's Nursery apron, but on him, it looked very different. "Declan! Hi. You work here?"

He grinned. "Nah, I'm all about fashion. Nothing says manly like an apron."

"It does look good on you." She turned away from him, like she knew she had to do, even if she didn't want to. Quickly, she filled a basket with the necessary herbs. Squaring her shoulders, she faced Mr. Neal. "I think I'm ready to check out."

He winked at her. "I'll let Declan take care of you." He said this as if he were doing her a favor instead of making things more complicated.

With her lips pressed into a straight line, she followed Declan down a sawdust-strewn path to the checkout counter. Memories of their few kisses tingled in the back of her mind. She wanted to dismiss them, but she couldn't. Part of her knew that kissing her brother shouldn't have felt so good, but what did she know? Declan was the only one she'd ever kissed. She wondered if she could kiss anyone else—just as an experiment—but she knew that wouldn't be fair. She didn't want to kiss anyone else, and besides it wouldn't be kind to kiss someone else when the one person she wanted to kiss was... her brother. She told herself to stop thinking about kissing.

No more kissing.

Ever?

"Is that all?" Declan asked.

Lizbet blinked at him and realized that he'd already rung up all her purchases. Her herbs were lined up in a

green cardboard box. "Yes. That's all." She hoped she sounded firm.

Declan watched her with an expectant look in his eyes.

She lifted her chin and met his gaze.

His lips twitched. "This is where you pay Mr. Neal for his plants. If it were up to me, I'd give them to you. But Mr. Neal has very firm ideas about receiving payment. Something to do with feeding his family."

Heat flushed up Lizbet's neck. "Of course. I don't know what I was thinking. I wasn't thinking..." Or, rather, she had been thinking about kissing... too much. That had to stop. Right now. To hide her blushing cheeks, she buried her head in her bag, taking much more time than she needed to pull out a twenty-dollar bill.

Declan glanced out at the empty parking lot. "I get off in a few minutes. If you don't mind waiting, I can drive you home."

"No!" Lizbet gathered up the box holding the herbs.

"Are you sure? It looks like it might rain."

"I'm waterproof," Lizbet said.

"But your box isn't."

"Well, that's silly, isn't it?" Lizbet's voice came out harsher than she intended. "Why hand out boxes that will fall apart in the rain when you live in the Pacific Northwest?"

"Most people just take them to their car—which is what you'd be doing if you let me drive you home."

Just then, lightning flashed, thunder cracked, and a few

fat raindrops began to fall. Lizbet's shoulders hunched. She knew she'd have to talk to Declan at some point. It might as well be now. "All right."

"Wow. You don't have to sound so sad about it."

"It's just..." She shot the sky another dark look, feeling betrayed by the weather. She started over. "There are things you don't know about me."

"And there are things you don't know about me."

She blew out a sigh.

"Do you want to wait in the car, or in here?" He nodded at the bench by the front door.

The stone bench was cold and hard. While she waited, she watched the rain and rehearsed what she could say to Declan. *I think your dad is my father.* Was she ready to share that information? She really felt like she had to talk to her mom first. How else could she know for sure? And if John Lamb was her dad, wouldn't that be something she should tell him before telling Declan? Declan, if he was like most, wouldn't want to hear about his dad having a long-term affair with anyone other than his mom—even if his parents were divorced. And if she and Declan were about the same age, wouldn't John have been married to Declan's mom around the time when Lizbet had been conceived? She shuddered. Thinking about her mom and John Lamb in that way gave her the willies.

A few minutes later, before she had found the right words, Declan showed up. "Ready?" he asked, holding

open the door and letting the rain and a cold breeze blow into the room.

He held a rain slicker over her head as they dashed through the parking lot to his Honda. After clicking the lock, he pulled the door open and waited for her to climb in and settle the box of herbs on her lap before slogging through the rain to the driver's side.

"Now, what is there about you that you think will scare me away?" he asked before putting the key in the ignition and turning on the engine.

The air from the vents blew cold, making Lizbet shiver. "It's not my secret to tell."

"Interesting... so there's a secret."

Knowing she'd piqued his interest, she decided she shouldn't have used that word. Maybe she shouldn't use any words. "Can you just drive me home?" she asked in a small voice.

He braced his hands on the steering wheel, but didn't put the car in gear. "No, I want to know the secret."

She opened her mouth, but when she couldn't find the right thing to say, she closed it again and fumbled for the door handle.

Declan reached out and put a hand on her wrist. "I'll drive you home. You don't have to share your secret... or anything else, if you don't want to."

She saw the hurt in his expression. "Thank you."

He pressed his lips together, put the car in reverse, and eased out of the parking lot.

After a few minutes, the heater kicked in and the air turned warm but the icy silence left Lizbet cold. She wanted to say something, anything, that would soften the look on Declan's face or loosen the tension between them, but she didn't know how so she said nothing until they pulled up to the ranch. "I think, in time, you'll see I'm right about this," she said while still hoping she was wrong.

Declan slammed through the door. He didn't mean to. He could blame the door quivering in its frame on the wind. It had helped. Sort of.

His dad looked up from his computer, registered Declan's expression, and returned to the NBA playoffs.

Declan snagged a Twinkie off the counter and headed for his room. His phone buzzed with a text. He waited until he was flat on his back and eating his Twinkie before he reached for his phone and saw the message was from Nicole.

Did you know that the Duke Lemur Center is the largest sanctuary for prosimian primates in the world?

He didn't know how to respond. Was a simple wow enough to be considered polite? Would it be rude to be honest and ask who cares? But maybe thinking about Nicole and lemurs would be better than dwelling on Lizbet and her secrets. Why did she have to lie to him? Why not just say she wasn't interested? For a distraction, he looked up the Lemur Center on the Internet.

According to Wikipedia, the lemurs occasionally escape from their natural habitat enclosures, he texted Nicole.

Things can get wild in Durham, Nicole shot back.

Okay. He really didn't know what to do with that. Declan polished off the Twinkie, changed out of his work clothes, grabbed his basketball, and headed for the door.

"Where are you going?" his dad asked.

Declan paused, his hand on the door. "Shoot some hoops."

"In the rain?"

Declan swore.

His dad raised his eyebrows. "You want to talk about it?"

"About what?" Declan growled.

"About why you need to shoot hoops in the rain?"

Declan dropped the ball, kicked it to a corner of the mudroom, and looked in the pantry for something other than a Twinkie. He sat down at the table with a bag of barbeque chips. "You've known the Westmoors for a long time—what do you think of Lizbet and her mom?"

His dad's face drained of color and his gaze skittered toward his computer. It was the NBA playoffs and the Lakers were ahead by twenty. "Why do you ask?"

"Lizbet... I don't get her."

His dad chuckled. "Okay, that's your problem right there."

"What?"

"You aren't meant to 'get' her. No one 'gets' anyone else, but especially not her."

"Why do you say 'especially not her'? What's so special about her?"

His dad pushed the laptop away. "You tell me."

Declan popped open the bag of chips and buried his hand in it. "I can't." After chewing but not tasting a few chips, he said, "Why would her mom live on a deserted island? That's bound to make anyone strange, isn't it?"

"I'm sure she had her reasons."

Declan slowly set down the bag of chips. "Why did you say it like that?"

His dad struggled to make his expression blank. "Like what?"

Declan shook a chip in his dad's face. "Like you know what her reasons are! You've known the family for years. How well did you know Daugherty? Did you ever meet Lizbet?"

John sighed. "I've known Daugherty since high school. She and your mom both went to North Coast Academy."

"Yeah, so what happened? What made her go off her rocker?"

He shook his head. "I never said she went off her rocker."

"But you knew where she was? This whole time, her family thought she was missing—even dead—and you said nothing?"

"You're jumping to conclusions." John held up his hands. "I never said that! You're reading things into this."

Declan slammed the table so hard his palms stung. "That's it! Lizbet changed the moment she saw you!" He squinted at his dad. "What did you do?"

"I didn't do anything! Listen, Daugherty had her secrets. And just like everyone else, I don't know where she's been or who she's been hiding from all these years. End of story."

Declan leaned back in his chair and folded his arms. "Whoa. That is not the end of the story. That sounds like the beginning of a story."

"You're right. We don't know how the story will end." John's voice sounded bleak.

"But you know how it started, right?"

John shook his head. "I really don't. I'm not sure anyone does. Even Daugherty."

"Why don't you tell me what you do know?"

From Declan's Research
Herbology- Herbalism. Herbalism is a
traditional medicinal or folk medicine
practice based on the use of
plants and plant extracts.

Chapter Fourteen

While Lizbet crushed the basil leaves and ground the ginger root, she thought about Mr. Neal talking to his plants. Was it so very different from her talking to animals? Did it cause the plants pain when she pulled off their leaves? If she tried to pull a whisker, or any other body part, off an animal, they would cry. But maybe for a plant, losing a leaf was like losing a hair or shedding skin. She considered the tiny leaf beneath her pestle. "Thanks, anyway," she murmured.

"Who are you talking to?"

Lizbet shot a surprised glance over her shoulder at Josie. Even though Josie had moved in several days ago, she and Lizbet had rarely crossed paths. Josie worked long hours, and seemed to be about as interested in being at the ranch as Elizabeth and Lizbet were to have her there.

"You," Lizbet said.

"You're thanking me?" Josie went to the cupboard, pulled out a mug, and shuffled to the coffeemaker. She'd changed out of her work clothes into a pair of slouchy sweats. Instead of heels, she wore fluffy pink socks, which made her seem like a totally different person.

"For letting me stay."

"Not my choice," Josie grumbled, letting Lizbet know that if she had been given a choice, Lizbet would be staying elsewhere.

Lizbet ground the rosemary and thyme with such force her arm began to ache.

"What are you doing?" Josie asked.

"Making a poultice for my mom," Lizbet said without looking up.

"Are you going to feed it to her?"

"No, I'm going to put it on her."

Josie shook her head, turned her back on Lizbet, and stared at the coffeemaker as if the power of her stare could make it brew faster. She spoke so quietly that Lizbet could barely hear her over the whoosh and swirl of the machine. "When I find out you are not my sister's daughter, you and your creepy cat will be out of here so fast your head will spin."

Lizbet didn't know how to respond so, feeling cowardly, she pretended she hadn't heard, but inside, she thought, *If I am not my mother's daughter, it will be a relief to know I'm not a blood relation to you.* She finished grinding the herbs, wiped her hands on the apron she'd borrowed from Elizabeth, and with shaking hands she poured the poultice into a glass jar. After cleaning up her workspace, she left the kitchen without a backward glance.

Outside, the cold air stung her face. The sun hovered on the mountaintop, settling into the trees and threatening to disappear. The jar containing the poultice felt heavy in her hand. She needed to take it to her mom but she didn't want to ask Matias for another ride and she wasn't sure where Elizabeth was. Of course, finding her was as easy as asking a bird, but the creeping feeling on the back of her neck warned her that Josie might still be watching. She strode for the barn.

There, in the dim light, the being-watched skin-pricking sensation eased but the tightness in her spine remained. Would she ever feel comfortable living with Josie? If her mom were awake, she could prove that Lizbet was her daughter. But without her mom, Lizbet had no proof. Did she blame Josie for being suspicious? No, not really. According to Tennyson, even the police had suspected her.

Lizbet shivered and moved deeper into the barn, out of the path of the cold breeze blowing through the open door. She spotted Elizabeth sitting on a hay bale, looking pale and dazed.

"Elizabeth? Are you okay?"

She nodded. "I'm fine, just a little shaken."

"Are you sure? Because you don't look so fine."

Elizabeth pointed at a large metal pulley system lying in the middle of the wooden floor. Lizbet recognized it as the device used for hoisting hay bales to the loft. The metal lifter was like a pitchfork attached to a rope with eighteen-inch curved tines with pointy ends. The pulley was a steel contraption about the size of a small microwave. It had to weight about thirty pounds. Normally, it hung harmlessly from the rafters. Since storing hay was typically done in the fall, Lizbet hadn't seen the pulley in action.

"What happened?"

"This fell." Elizabeth's voice quivered. "If it wasn't for an owl darting at me, it would have hit me."

"An owl? In the middle of the day?"

Elizabeth rubbed her eyes, looking tired. "It was a freak accident... but..."

Lizbet reached for Elizabeth's hand. "Come on, I'll make you some tea."

Elizabeth mutely nodded and followed Lizbet into the house.

Lucy had joined Josie in the kitchen. While both women fussed over Elizabeth, Josie shot Lizbet poisonous looks as if she were somehow to blame.

"Tell us exactly what happened," Josie said, hovering over her mom.

"I'll make some tea," Lizbet said.

"No!" Josie barked. "Lucy, you do it."

Did Josie think Lizbet would try and poison them? Lizbet sank into a chair, overwhelmed by Josie's hostility. Did she really think that Lizbet would try to harm Elizabeth? Why would she do that?

"Well, I was passing through the barn, heading for the stables, when the pulley system fell," Elizabeth said in quivering voice. "It was so close I felt the air whoosh around me. If it wasn't for a large white owl, it would have fallen on my head." Elizabeth shivered.

Lucy made the sign of the cross over her heart while she filled the teapot with water. "In many cultures, owls are a harbinger of death," Lucy said.

"Not helpful," Josie muttered.

"But this owl saved my life," Elizabeth pointed out.

"And where were you when all this happened?" Josie asked Lizbet.

"I came in afterwards. I found Elizabeth sitting on a hay bale."

Josie sniffed.

A knocking on the door interrupted them. Lucy went to answer it.

Declan stood on the back porch, his jaw tense and his eyes full of determination. He smiled and nodded at the other women in the room, but when he turned to Lizbet the resolute look returned. "Can I talk to you?"

"Sure," Lizbet said slowly, rising from her chair when Declan nodded his head outside.

"I wonder what that's all about," Josie said.

Lizbet didn't mind closing the door on Josie, but she was worried about Elizabeth.

"Let's go where no one can overhear us," Declan said.

Lizbet followed his gaze to the fields where Matias was working with a small cluster of horses. She was sure he was out of earshot, but she wondered if Declan wanted him out of eyesight, as well.

"Let's go to the barn," she said. "I want to see something there, anyway."

He silently followed her through the tall grass and the cavernous barn doors. She felt keenly aware of him behind her as she made her way to the center of the barn to gaze at the wooden beams running across the ceiling.

"What are you looking for?" Declan ask, his gaze following hers.

"Today, the pulley for the hay lift fell and nearly landed on Elizabeth. It really shook her up." From such a great distance, it was hard to see anything. "It could have been an accident, but it seems really coincidental." She placed her hands on her hips and frowned at the ceiling. "I have to get up there."

Declan shrugged and followed her to the ladder running up the side of the back wall. He held it for her while she climbed to the loft before coming after her. Chinks of sunlight filtered through the wooden slats and dust motes flitted through the air.

Lizbet went to inspect the scars left behind on the beams where, until just recently, the pulley had hung. She couldn't get directly beneath the beams because of the gaping hole that allowed the hay bales to pass through. "I still can't tell anything," she said.

"What were you hoping to find?"

"Evidence of tampering, of course."

He reached out and rubbed her back. "Do you think it's possible your experience with your mom has made you... cautious?"

She peered at him. "You were going to say paranoid, weren't you?"

He folded his arms and met her gaze. "How reasonable is it to assume that someone snuck into the barn and waited until Elizabeth walked by before dropping a pulley system on her head? Why would anyone do that? What could they stand to gain?"

"Josie and a man named Gaylord Godwin want to turn the ranch into a resort."

Declan blanched. "Do you know Godwin?"

"No, but..."

"Well, I do. He's my stepfather."

"Oh, Declan... I'm sorry. I didn't mean to—"

He cut her off. "I'm sorry, too—that he's my stepfather. But even though I don't like him, I know that he would never try and kill your grandmother, or anyone for that matter, to build a hotel."

"You don't like him?"

"No. But how I feel about him doesn't really matter. The point is, he's smart. And he's rich. He would never risk a prison sentence for an attempted murder just to build a resort."

Lizbet sat down on a hay bale. It let out a huff of dust as if to complain.

"Do you honestly think Josie would try and kill her own mother?"

"No," Lizbet said slowly.

Declan picked out a hay bale across from her and sat so close their knees almost touched. "So—who does that leave? Who would want to hurt Elizabeth and why?"

"I don't know."

He nodded and looked pleased with himself. "It was a freak accident."

"Maybe..." Lizbet drew out the word. Maybe she had to concede that her mother's warnings still rang in her head. Maybe she couldn't be trusting because of the things her mother had taught her from an early age. Would she always see boogeymen around every corner and monsters beneath every bed? Was she doomed to a life of paranoia? Sure, Declan could call it being cautious, but wasn't that just a kind word for anxious and delusional? Did she really want to be like her mother and spend her life cloistered on a deserted island? Feeling slightly ill, she pressed her hand against her forehead.

Declan stretched out his hand and placed it on her knee. She gazed at it, wondering what to say that hadn't already been said. He squeezed her knee softly.

"I need to talk to you about something," he said, his voice soft.

She nodded, waiting. He didn't remove his hand, and she didn't ask him to, guessing that siblings could and would touch each other's knees.

"My dad wants to meet you."

"What?" She bounced up, turned her back on him, and ran her fingers through her hair. "Why?"

He stood and placed a hand on her shoulder. "He wants to meet Daugherty's daughter."

"Why?" Lizbet asked, her throat tight.

"I think you know why. He didn't know about you."

She blew out a breath, knowing that she should have foreseen this, knowing that John was right. So why did this feel like a betrayal to her mom? She must have had her reasons for keeping John away. She slowly turned back to Declan and was surprised by his nearness.

He met her gaze with an intense blue-eyed stare. "We're not siblings."

"You can't know that."

"My dad insists it's impossible—and I believe him. But he's still willing to take a paternity test, if you are, even though his affair with your mom, according to him, was all in his head."

"All in his head?" Her thoughts returned to that first stormy night and the ginger root tea.

"But I know we're not siblings. Brothers and sisters don't feel like this." His hand came up to graze her cheek.

She pulled away. "You can't know that," she said with a tight voice. "Neither one of us can. We're both only children."

He grinned.

"What?"

"Don't you see? If we're siblings, we can't be only children. You know as well as I do we're not related." He drew closer, pinning the backs of her legs against a hay bale. "I really want to kiss you," he said in a hot breath.

"It's a really bad idea," she said.

"Why?"

"Because once we start, I'm not sure we'd be able to stop." She back-stepped over the hay bale and maneuvered away from the gaping hole in the center of the loft. "Why don't you tell me about my mom and your dad? You must have talked to him about it."

Declan nodded. "But that's his story to tell, not mine. He wants to meet you. He didn't know you existed. He admitted to fantasizing about your mom, but that's it."

She watched his face. "That's not it, is it? And you know it."

Suspicion flickered over his expression. "What do you know?"

She sighed. "I know how to make ginger root tea."

"How was that?"

"Ginger root tea. I'll make you some sometime."

"I think I'll pass."

"That's probably wise."

"Do you want to know what's not wise?" He didn't wait for her to answer. "Hanging out here with you and not kissing you. Come on, let's go meet my dad." He held out his hand and she took it.

John stood in front of the stovetop stirring a simmering pan of spaghetti sauce. The room that was kitchen, living room, and entry hall all rolled into one smelled of roasting garlic. Declan could tell that Lizbet was not only hungry, but also impressed.

While he believed his dad's story, he could, if he imagined it, see the resemblance between him and Lizbet. They were both dark with deep green eyes and thick nearly-black hair, but Lizbet was tiny while John had quarterback shoulders, a barrel chest, and burly muscles.

John put down his spatula, wiped his hands on his jeans, and came to give Lizbet a brief hug. He pulled away and looked into her eyes. "I don't see it," he said slowly. After giving a mental shrug, he returned to his place behind the stove. "I was hoping you would come, so I made us dinner." He nodded at the kitchen table.

Declan smiled that his dad had even found a tablecloth in some dark corner of the linen closet. The books, newspapers, and books of logic puzzles that normally hung out on the table had been piled up on the counter and replaced with three place settings with full sets of silverware and even matching glasses. Maybe Lizbet wasn't John's daughter, but he was still obviously trying to make a good impression.

"Sit!" John said, waving at the table. He picked up a pair of oven mitts that looked like salmon and went to the oven to check on the garlic bread. A heavenly smell wafted across the room.

Declan waited for Lizbet to sit before he pulled out a chair next to her.

"I know you have questions," John said as he carried the garlic bread to the table. "But so do I. And I figured we all need to eat, so..."

"This is great," Lizbet said. "Is there anything I can do to help?"

"No, just be prepared to be peppered with questions," John said over his shoulder as he headed back to the stove for the pasta pot.

When everyone was settled at the table and each had heaping piles of spaghetti, John began. "The first time... I won't call it a fantasy." He took a long swallow of red wine before carefully choosing his next words. "Honestly, I don't know what to call it." He shook his head. "Okay, here's

what happened. One day shortly after my divorce, I went fishing out on the Sound. The weather was brooding, and I knew a storm could start at any moment, but I didn't care. It suited my mood. Back then, I was... miserable." He rubbed a tired hand over his face. "Anyway, I got caught in a storm and I battled the waves and wind for what seemed like hours. I must have passed out because I woke the next day in the middle of Haradan Strait. The Sound was calm, the air clear, and my boat was none the worse for the storm. My head was buzzed, but other than that I was fine." He cocked an eyebrow at Lizbet. "Is there anything you want to add to that story?"

Lizbet pushed her spaghetti around her plate with her fork, suddenly ashamed of her mom. "I could, but I want to hear about your relationship with my mom."

John sighed. "All right. I'll go first, but after that, I want answers."

Lizbet smiled. "I'll answer what I can, but you might be disappointed."

"If you're telling me that my... episodes... with Daugherty were real, I promise you, I won't be disappointed."

Lizbet swallowed hard. "Then you'll be happy to know that you visited the island and my mom many times."

John put down his fork. "How is that possible?"

"Ginger root tea. It makes people forget."

"All those dreams... are you telling me they were all real?"

Lizbet shrugged. "I have no way of knowing. You'll have to ask my mom."

"How is it I never met you? If what you're telling me is true, I must have been to the island a hundred times."

Lizbet smiled. "Not quite a hundred."

"Often, though..."

"Did you ever think about telling anyone?"

John groaned, put down his fork and gazed at Lizbet. "That's the worst question. The one I've struggled with for years. But how could I?" He picked up his glass and took a quick swallow of water. "As you know, your family has been friends with the Forsyths for years. Gloria, my ex-wife, and Daugherty went to North Coast Academy together, and while they weren't close, they were friends. I met Daugherty at weddings, parties, and social occasions only a few times before her disappearance."

Lizbet leaned forward and braced her elbows on the table, her food completely forgotten. "Do you know what happened? Why she disappeared?"

"I don't. And I'm pretty sure no one else does either, including your mom."

"What do you mean?"

"In my dreams, she had amnesia. I found her on a wild night. I'd been out fishing and the storm caught me completely by surprise. I was looking for shelter and I spotted the light of the cottage. My boat nearly capsized, and I almost drowned. My clothes were soaked, and I'd

hit my head." He chuckled. "I think if I hadn't been so pathetic she would never have let me in."

"But she did."

"But first she made me swear that I'd never tell or reveal her whereabouts. At that point, I would have promised anything to anyone for a warm fire and dry clothes. She let me in and bandaged up my head, but refused to answer my questions. After a while, I realized that she wasn't answering the questions not only because she didn't want to, but also because she didn't know the answers. She gave me her bed that night and the next morning, as I said, I was lying on the floor of my boat in the middle of the Sound. I had no proof that she even existed. At that time, I wasn't even sure if she was Daugherty. I went back a few days later, but once again, I couldn't find her. I thought it was all a dream. A dream I repeatedly enjoyed."

Lizbet slowly picked up her fork and scooted spaghetti around her plate. "Why do you think she was the way she was?"

John shook his head. "Who's to say? It was almost like she was brainwashed. She was like a frightened child." He twirled noodles around his fork. "Now it's your turn. Tell me what you know about your mom."

Lizbet told him about her life on the island—the simplicity and the harsh reality of the biting cold, the temperamental wood stove, and the monotony of eating home-canned vegetables for every meal. And the secret hope she'd nurtured for years that John was her father.

"I'm happy to pay for a paternity test if you'd like, but I can assure you, your mother and I didn't have that sort of relationship. In time, we became friends. But that's it."

Lizbet cocked her eyebrow at him.

"Okay, that's not completely it," he admitted after a moment, "but remember, I thought your mom was a figment of my imagination and the island was my personal, delusional refuge."

Lizbet tightened her hold on her glass of water, feeling the condensation pooling around her fingers. It couldn't dampen her resolve to help her mom. "Can you drive me to visit my mom?" she asked Declan.

"I would be happy to do that," John said. "If you don't mind, I would love to see her."

They made arrangements to visit the hospital the next day.

When Lizbet came downstairs the next morning, she found both Elizabeth and Josie in the kitchen. A brittle, icy silence hung between them. She felt as if she'd interrupted a conversation that bordered on an argument neither intended to lose. Scooping up her poultice, Lizbet explained her plan to go to the hospital with John Lamb. Elizabeth greeted the news with an appreciative smile, while Josie slanted her a suspicious glance. Lizbet bundled the poultice into the basket she generally used to carry

Tennyson, tucked it under her arm, and left. She'd rather wait for John in the early spring sunshine than in the hostile kitchen.

She wondered how long Josie and Elizabeth had been warring. If she had to guess, she would say that their conflict had started about the time Josie first expressed her opinion. So, as soon as she had learned to wave a fat baby fist and squeal. She'd probably been squealing ever since.

Not that Josie was completely in the wrong. Even if it wasn't here yet, there would soon come a time when Elizabeth shouldn't be living on the ranch alone—for her own safety as well as her animals. She was increasingly forgetful and accident prone. But Lizbet also suspected Josie's motives had a heaping helping of greed mixed in with concern for her mother.

The sun sparkled on the tops of the trees to the east. Somewhere, church bells rang. Lizbet loved how the forest circling the ranch made it feel isolated and otherworldly while in reality, it was just a stone's throw from the highway that led to East End. That was probably one of the things that made it an ideal location for a resort.

A crunch of gravel in the driveway announced John's arrival. Lizbet watched his Corolla roll her way and clutched the basket. She had mixed feelings about not being his daughter. For so many years, he'd played the role of father in her head and it was hard to let that go. He was such a kind man, she understood exactly why her

mother and Declan loved him so much. She wanted to love him, too, and she felt sure, if given the chance, she would.

But if not being his daughter meant she could kiss Declan... Heat rose in her cheeks, and she told herself she shouldn't be thinking about kissing Declan while sharing space with his father. She spotted Declan in the passenger seat and her heart beat faster. Would he always have this effect on her? Even if she learned that John was mistaken, or lying, and that Declan was her brother?

Maybe Declan was right, a sibling couldn't feel the way she did for him. Should she insist on the paternity test? Her Internet research had told her that such a test wasn't cheap, and John didn't live like a man with oodles of money.

The Corolla pulled up beside her, and she climbed into the back seat. The warmth in the car matched John and Declan's smiles and greetings. She slowly began to thaw, realizing how chilly the ranch had been with Josie and Elizabeth.

When his dad peeled away from them in the hospital lobby, Declan couldn't hide his surprise.

"Gotta get something," John mumbled with flushed cheeks.

"What?" Declan asked.

"Room 345, right?" John asked, twisting his hands.

Lizbet nodded.

"I'll be right up, okay?" John said, looking embarrassed and sheepish.

This was a side of his dad Declan hadn't seen before. He didn't like it.

Lizbet nudged him. "Do you want to check in on your grandfather?"

Declan shrugged.

Lizbet tucked her hand around his arm and gently steered him to the bank of elevators.

"Where's he going?" Declan asked.

"He hasn't seen her in several months. Maybe he wants to check his hair—you know, look his best." Lizbet pressed the elevator button and the doors slid open.

"Look his best? She's in a coma!"

"Maybe she'll wake up when she sees him."

"Like Sleeping Beauty? This isn't a fairy tale."

Lizbet squeezed his arm. "Life can be as magical as you make it."

Declan didn't respond because he didn't want to argue with her. He knew Lizbet saw the world differently than him. He blamed her wacky upbringing and her nearly total immersion in books. Real life didn't come with a fairy godmother or guarantee a happy ending. She'd learn that soon enough.

Declan pressed the elevator button and it carried them to the fifth floor where his grandfather lay. But when they got there, the room was empty. The thumping in his chest surprised him. He had never met his grandfather. The man was a stranger to him, so why did his sudden disappearance rattle him?

Lizbet reached for his hand and gave it a reassuring squeeze. Together, they stopped a short nurse with spiky dark hair.

"My grandfather. Frank Forsythe, in 511. What happened?" Declan's question came out in short staccato breaths.

"Frank? He was discharged yesterday. The doctors were hesitant to let him go but, of course, we can't keep him against his will."

Declan's throat clenched. "Do you think he's okay on his own?"

The nurse smiled and leaned forward to say in a low, conspiratorial tone, "Want my honest opinion? He'll be fine. He's got enough spunk in him to light up a warehouse. It's the morose, docile ones we need to worry about."

A weight shifted off Declan's chest. He still had time. He could still meet this man his parents both despised, for different reasons, who had the energy to light up warehouses. He wondered why he wanted to know him. Was it just curiosity? Or was there something more?

Declan turned to Lizbet. She stood beside him, but angled away, her attention fastened on a small bird on the other side of a large window. She cocked her head, as if listening to the small bird's chirping, before dropping his hand.

"I need to see my mom," she said, her voice tight.

From Declan's Research
"Be praised, my Lord, through Brother Fire, through
whom you brighten the night. He is beautiful and
cheerful, and powerful and strong."
—Francis of Assisi

Chapter Fifteen

John stood by the hospital bed, holding a large bouquet of yellow roses. He wore a dazed look on his face. "She spoke to me."

Lizbet rushed to her mom's bedside and picked up her hand. "Mom?"

Her mom didn't answer with words, but she squeezed Lizbet's hand.

"Mom!" Lizbet shook her.

Declan placed his hands on Lizbet's shoulders, calming her. "Don't. She'll come around."

Lizbet whirled on John, suddenly hating him, jealous that he would be the first one her mom would choose to speak to. "What did she say?"

"Her speech was garbled, but I think she said, 'My name is Daugherty,' which is interesting because when I imagined her on the island, she always insisted her name was Rose."

Lizbet gazed into her mom's pale face. Her light brown lashes fanned her cheeks. Light gray smudges lined her eyes but her cheeks were a faded pink and her lips had lost their bloodless tone. Hope welled in Lizbet's chest. "Do you think... Is it possible her memory has returned?" That would answer so many questions.

"I don't know. I'm not sure if she recognized me or not."

Lizbet sank into a chair, determined not to leave again until her mom woke. "You guys can go. I'm going to stay here."

John awkwardly patted her shoulder. "I've heard that often when people wake from a coma they go through a dreamlike stage where they suffer from nightmares and delusions. This might be difficult to watch."

Lizbet shook her head, refusing to be dissuaded. "I'm not leaving. I never should have left. I should have stayed here in the first place."

"She wouldn't have wanted that," Declan said.

"You don't even know her," Lizbet spat out. "How can you say what she would or would not have wanted?"

"Daugherty is loving and compassionate." John kept, his voice low and calm as if he were trying to soothe a wounded animal. "She would want what's best for her daughter. She'd want you to be focusing on your studies, preparing for you future."

"With my mom, my future was on the island with her. She didn't—"

John cut her off. "That wasn't the Daugherty I knew—"

Lizbet bounced to her feet. "Are you saying that you knew her better than me?"

"No, not at all," John said, still using his pacifying and yet irritating voice. "But I have known her longer."

Lizbet's mom made a horrifying gurgling scream, effectively curtailing the argument. Doctors and nurses rushed into the room and monitors began beeping and flashing as Lizbet's mom thrashed and tried to pull the IVs out of her skin. A nurse shooed Lizbet, Declan, and John out of the room.

"You could stay," the nurse said once she had them in the hall, away from the commotion. "But I think it would be best if you didn't witness this. Sometimes coma patients are completely out of their minds during this stage."

Lizbet tried to shut out her mom's screams, but she couldn't. She moved for the door, but Declan took her hand. "Maybe I can help," Lizbet said, searching his eyes and seeing only compassion.

"No, sweetie," the nurse said. "These vivid nightmares and disturbing hallucinations are the brain's way of trying to make sense of what's happening. They say that for some, it can take longer to heal from the delusions than from any physical injuries. This isn't something you should witness."

As her mother's screams continued, Lizbet felt more and more desperate.

"We should call Elizabeth," John said, pulling out his phone.

"She won't be able to do anything, either," Declan said.

"She'll still want to know," Lizbet put in.

John handed her his phone. "Do you want to tell her?"

Lizbet took the phone and wandered over to a chair in the waiting room. She glanced around at the others sharing the sterile space. The orange upholstered chairs tried to look cheerful, but failed when mixed with the glaring white walls, drab artwork, and the blank, tired expressions of the people waiting for news of their loved ones.

When Elizabeth answered the phone, Lizbet filled her in on the situation.

Declan sat beside her, his hands between his knees. "I know you don't want to leave, but if listening to your mom is painful for me, it has to be murder for you. Do you want to go for a walk?"

"But what if—"

"My dad will call us." He laced his fingers through hers. "Please?"

She knew she should tell him no, just like she knew she shouldn't be holding his hand. But at that moment, she needed a hand to hold. She needed him. She let him lead her out of the building.

They walked a few blocks before turning onto a quiet street. Century-old mansions stood beneath giant maple, pine, and cedar trees. It seemed eons away from the bustling Queen Anne Center.

"Where are we?" Lizbet asked.

"The University District," Declan told her. "Mostly, this is where the professors live." He walked as if he had a destination, as if he wasn't just killing time.

"Are we going somewhere in particular?" Lizbet asked.

Declan didn't answer. But after a moment, he stopped in front of a large Tudor home surrounded by lilacs, dogwood, and sprawling rhododendrons. Light glinted through mullion windows. It seemed sad to her, because it looked like a home that should have had a family, but was eerily quiet. "My grandfather's house."

She would have continued to stare, but Declan pulled her away.

"Do you want to meet him?" Lizbet asked.

"I do, but only if he wants to meet me." He dropped her hand and shoved his own into his pockets.

"But he did want to meet you, remember?"

"Why didn't he call then? If he was healthy enough to get himself discharged from the hospital, he's well enough to pick up a phone."

"Maybe he doesn't know what to say."

Declan threw an arm over her shoulders and steered her back toward the hospital. "You think the best of everyone."

She dragged her feet, wanting to linger on the quiet street with its wide stretches of lawn and well-maintained flowerbeds. "Is that an accusation?"

"An observation," he said, matching his pace to hers.

She tucked her hand into his back pocket, telling herself that a sibling might do the same. Maybe, if she had to, she could wean herself away from him, but for right now she was glad to have him beside her. She had so very few people she could depend upon. He was someone she could trust. For now, at least.

Back at the hospital, they found John and Elizabeth eyeing each other from opposite sides of Lizbet's mom's hospital bed. Elizabeth motioned to Lizbet's mom's hand clasped in John's. "Is there something you need to tell me, Johnny?"

John cleared his throat. "I'm afraid it will… make you angry."

Elizabeth balled her hands and planted them on her hips. "I think I'm already angry!"

Declan took Lizbet's hand and pulled her out of the room and out of the combat zone. "I don't think this is going to go well for my dad," he whispered.

"You can hardly blame her for being mad." Lizbet matched his low tone. "All these years he let her believe her daughter was dead."

"He thought she was!"

So he said, Lizbet thought, keeping her opinion to herself and her hand tucked in Declan's back pocket.

On the drive home, Lizbet knew something was wrong as soon as Elizabeth's car crested the hill. A dark smudge of smoke mingled with gathering storm clouds and the sharp sent of burning pine permeated the air.

Elizabeth must have sensed it as well, because she pushed the Suburban faster and took the corners so fast Lizbet clutched her seatbelt with one hand and the car door handle with the other.

They rounded a turn. Lizbet and Elizabeth both gasped at the sight of orange flames licking the trees behind the farmhouse, spitting ash and embers to the sky, and threatening the lives of the horses kicking their legs in fear and panic in the pasture.

Billowing black smoke filled the sky and shaded the sun. A hot wind carried the ashes toward the mountains. Crimson streaks leapt upwards and shot through the twilight. Popping embers shot randomly in all directions.

Elizabeth darted from the car, but Lizbet caught her wrist and held her fast. The hungry fire blew through the woods, and Lizbet shared Elizabeth's worries about the animals and their homes, but she couldn't let her grandmother go into the barn. Above them, flaming cherry red ashes and embers flew, bursting in the darkening sky, some landed on trees and a number fell into the grass. Something exploded in the barn with a boom and the fire

surged white hot red. Lizbet fought Elizabeth until her arms ached.

"Let me go!" Elizabeth demanded.

Lizbet shook her. "You can't go in there! We need to call the fire department, if this spreads, you could lose your entire ranch!"

Elizabeth stopped struggling, nodded mutely, her eyes never leaving the fire destroying her beloved farm. Another crack and the barn's roof disappeared into the flames. The heat scorched the tears on Lizbet's cheeks. Smoke filled her eyes, lungs, and chest. Turning away from the oppressive heat, shaking, she realized she wasn't the same person that she'd been a few weeks ago. Before coming to the mainland, she'd been looking to her mom to define her life and create her path. Now, watching Elizabeth's passion potentially disappearing into flames, she knew her grandmother would risk her life to save her farm. Lizbeth needed to find a passion of her own.

Lizbet held both of her grandmother's arms and met and held her gaze. "You go to Hernandez's, warn them, and use their phone if they haven't already called the fire department."

Elizabeth shook her head. "I'll find a garden hose."

"No, I'll find the hose. You go to the Hernandez's. Take the car." Lizbet pulled her against her briefly, fighting her desire to argue. She gave up. "Be safe," she said.

With trembling fingers Lizbet pulled open the gate separating the orchard from the lawn. Running towards the house, she caught sight of Tennyson hiding beneath a giant fern. He cowered as she ran past. She stooped down to rescue him, but he darted away. She watched his tail disappear through the slats of the broken fence separating the pasture from the driveway.

She found the hose coiled beneath a rose bush on the side the house. The untended rose had grown spindly long legs with wicked thorns that scratched Lizbet's arms and caught hold of her T-shirt and skirt. The spigot burned her hands so badly she couldn't turn the water on. She found a large rake and tried to beat the faucet into the on position, but her efforts broke the handle. Tears welled in her eyes and stung her cheeks. The fire roared, embers snapped, and horses screamed. She longed to comfort them, but knew they wouldn't be calm until the fire was out.

And neither would she or Elizabeth.

The hose surged with water. Lizbet picked it up and went to confront the fire. Somewhere in the distance, sirens began to wail, letting her know she wasn't alone.

Hours later, while Lizbet soaked in a tub and rubbed lavender soap over her ashy skin, she half-listened to Josie's rantings through the floorboards.

"What happened?" Josie shrieked.

Someone, probably Elizabeth, murmured a reply.

"You can't continue to live here! It's not safe!"

More mumbling.

The conversation hushed momentarily.

"You don't even know her!" Josie yelled.

"And neither do you!" Elizabeth quipped back.

Lizbet sat up, knowing they were talking about her. What would she do if Josie won the argument? Lizbet was quite sure that someday she would. Lizbet couldn't continue to sponge off her grandmother. She needed a plan. And waiting for her mom to wake wasn't the answer.

Although she didn't want to go very far in case her mother did wake up.

Lizbet rubbed shampoo into her hair, hoping its fragrance could wash away the smoky smell. She tried to help out as much as she could, but she knew she didn't carry her weight around the ranch. Tomorrow, she decided as she lay back in the water, completely submerging, she would find a job.

Declan stood outside his mom's door with his hands shoved in his pockets. He had questions about his grandfather that only she could answer. But the one thought haunting him, the one he couldn't shake, was one he knew

his mom wouldn't be any help with. It was something he had to figure out on his own.

"Declan, my boy!" Godwin rounded the corner with Rufus at his side.

Declan hated being called Godwin's boy. For one thing, his birthday and legal adulthood were just weeks away, and for another, he didn't want to belong to Godwin in any way.

"To what do we owe the pleasure?" Godwin asked. "Have you come to meditate on our porch?"

"No," Declan said, trying not to sound annoyed. "Is my mom here?"

Godwin looked at his watch. "I'm afraid not. She's hosting an open house at the Vances' property until five. Is there something I can do for you?"

"Did you know my grandfather checked out of the hospital?"

Godwin's eyes sparked with interest. "Your mother will want to know. Thanks for keeping us abreast of the situation."

Abreast? Who talks like that? "Uh, sure. So, if I came back at five do you think my mom will be here?"

Godwin looked at his watch again. "We're dining with the Greens at seven."

Ever since Godwin had married his mom, Declan had felt like he needed an appointment to speak with her. He tried to remember if this had always been the case or if Godwin had monopolized her life, leaving her little time or room for her son.

"You're welcome to stay here and wait. You could even move inside if standing on the porch grows stale."

And now he felt like a loaf of bread. Better move before he got stale... or grew mold. Declan shoved his hands into his pockets. "Can you tell her I came by?"

"Sure thing, sport."

Sport? He liked being called sport almost as much as he liked being Godwin's boy. A shiver crawled down his back as he made his way to the Honda as fast as he could without actually breaking into a jog.

Finding a job was a lot harder than Lizbet had thought it'd it would be. When a barrel-shaped man in Mirna's Café explained to her she'd need a social security card before he could hire her, and to get one of those she'd need a birth certificate, she returned to the ranch tired and discouraged.

When she found Elizabeth sitting at the table with her head buried in her arms, Lizbet knew she wasn't the only one having a bad day. Elizabeth's shoulders shook with sobs. Lizbet didn't know exactly what had happened, but she guessed it somehow involved Josie and the ranch.

But then again, Elizabeth could be upset about Lizbet's mother. Maybe while she was gone, Elizabeth had received bad news. Maybe her mom had taken a turn for the worse, although for things to get any worse... Lizbet's heart

clenched. She couldn't jump to conclusions. She couldn't think about her mother dying. It had been days since her mother had woken from her coma only to slip back into it.

"Would you like some tea?" Lizbet asked, gently laying her hand on Elizabeth's quivering back, trying to stem her own panic.

Slowly, Elizabeth lifted her head. "I didn't hear you come in." Elizabeth used both hands to wipe away her tears. "I'm sorry you have to see me like this."

"I'm sorry you're so sad." Lizbet filled the teapot with water, pulled the teabags from the cupboard, and set two mugs on the counter, knowing that after Elizabeth shared her news, she, Lizbet, would also likely need some tea.

"Josie... she's threatening to have me declared mentally incompetent if I won't leave the ranch."

Relief washed through Lizbet. She was so grateful the news wasn't about her mom it took a few moments to register the implications of what Elizabeth was saying. She sat at the table beside Elizabeth and tried to process. "What exactly does that mean?"

"It means that she blames me for the fire. She's been saying for a long time that I shouldn't be living here alone."

"But you're not alone. I'm here."

A scowl settled over Elizabeth's forehead. "That argument isn't going to score any points with Josie. I'm not exactly sure my safety is Josie's paramount concern."

Lizbet put her hand over Elizabeth's and gave it a squeeze. "I think she loves you very much. She just doesn't know how to express it."

Elizabeth snorted. "I think she loves money more."

"That's not true." Lizbet thought about the fire. Most of the damage was to an old outbuilding that had been burned down to stubs and beams and the barn. An ember or two had landed on the back corner of the house, scorching that side of the roof.

"Do you know how the fire started?"

Elizabeth shook her head. "I don't have a clue."

"What did the firemen say?"

"The fire marshal suggested the old cans of paint and turpentine I stored in that building might be responsible."

The teapot began to squeal and Lizbet went to retrieve it. "But what would strike a spark? It wasn't at all warm yesterday. I find it hard to believe the cans would just explode. You didn't light a match out there, did you?"

Elizabeth huffed. "Of course not! But there may have been some frayed electrical wiring."

"Then I don't see how this can be your fault."

"Well, what you and I see might not be all that relevant. Josie will take me to a judge and have me declared mentally incompetent if I don't move off the ranch."

"But where will you go?"

"To Josie's."

"I thought... the rodents..."

Elizabeth sighed. "She checked her security camera's footage. There hasn't been any sign of mice or rats since she moved out." Elizabeth narrowed her eyes. "And she thinks I'm mentally incompetent!"

"You're moving into her condo?"

Elizabeth nodded. "She'll get tired of me plenty soon and send me packing. This is where I belong. She just needs to learn that."

Lizbet thought that since Elizabeth had lived on the ranch Josie's entire life that Josie should have learned that lesson a long time ago.

Elizabeth cocked her head at Lizbet. "Will you stay here and take care of the animals while I'm gone? I'll come by every afternoon."

"Of course." Where else would she go?

Josie came to collect Elizabeth and a hastily packed suitcase an hour later. Lizbet carried the suitcase down the steps and to the driveway where Josie stood waiting beside her BMW, jiggling her keys and looking impatient.

Elizabeth drew Lizbet into a tight hug. "It won't be so very different. I'll come out every day while Josie's at work."

"Mother." Josie breathed out a sigh.

Elizabeth slowly pulled away from Lizbet. "You have the list I made."

"I do."

"And remember the chickens—"

"Like music. Yes, I know."

"But not loud songs. No rock 'n' roll. It has to be pleasing to them. They're gentle spirits. Anything too raucous and they won't be able to lay. And Trotter..."

"Keep him away from the apple tree."

"Yes!" Elizabeth pointed a finger in Lizbet's face. "Or else you'll have a holy mess on your boot."

"Got it."

"I'll be here first thing tomorrow morning," Elizabeth promised.

"Mother, let's go." Josie took the suitcase out of Lizbet's hand, tossed it into the trunk of her car, and opened the passenger door for Elizabeth.

Elizabeth climbed in, the door slammed shut, and Josie rounded the car for the driver's side. As if as acting on a last-minute thought, she pocketed the car keys and strode toward the porch. Placing her hands on her hips, she lifted her chin and confronted Lizbet.

"In two weeks, this property will be sold. I'm giving you fair warning. You need to get your pretty little assets together and find someone else to feed, house, and clothe you. My mother is done providing your free ride."

Lizbet folded her arms, trying to protect herself from Josie's hostility. She knew Josie's words wouldn't hurt so badly if they weren't laden with truth.

Lizbet still had thousands of dollars from her mother's safe so she didn't have to worry. Using the bike she found in the shed, she could easily ride into town for food and

other necessities. Elizabeth, true to her word, drove out to the ranch every day. Lizbet made her breakfast, lunch, and dinner. Her life wasn't really so different from before, but the long and lonely nights left her empty.

It seemed strange to her, because she had spent so many years with just her mom, but as the days drew on, she found herself increasingly restless. She filled her evenings with school work, religiously studying for the exams Matias told her she would need to pass to get into college. She spent the days caring for the animals and the garden, and overseeing the repairs to the barn and house. A team of gardeners had also spiffed up the flowerbeds and lawns and a painting crew had touched up the trim on the house, barn, and fences. On the day the workmen finished their magic and loaded up their tools, Josie arrived.

"We're going to have a party," she announced.

"A party?" Lizbet wondered who Josie would invite. She seemed an unlikely person to have any friends.

"I've already sent out the invitations. You," she announced, "are not invited."

Lizbet just raised her eyebrow, because this was fine with her. If Josie did have friends, Lizbet was pretty sure she wouldn't like them. "Do you want me to hide in the barn with the animals?"

"No, I want to show off the horses. You can hang in your room."

Lizbet thought of all the places Josie could hang, but since she was living on the ranch rent-free, she kept her mouth shut.

"It's not only friends she invited," Tennyson told her later that night when they lay in bed. Lizbet looked up from her textbook while Tennyson rolled onto his back, stretching. *"I'm not sure she has any of those. She's invited investors,"* Tennyson continued. *"It will be a catered affair with a tent set up on the front lawn. A full bar. An open grill with a choice of salmon, steak, or chicken."* The cat licked his paw.

"You intend on going, don't you?" Lizbet's suspicions mounted while she gazed at the lounging cat.

"You betcha!" Tennyson's tail swished.

Lizbet's lips twitched, hiding a smile. "You, my dear friend, won't be welcome."

"That makes it more fun!"

Lizbet softly laughed, then hushed as an awful idea occurred to her. An awesome and awful idea.

"Ah," Tennyson purred, *"I knew you would get there eventually."*

"We couldn't..." Lizbet said, her voice escaping in a low breath.

"Why not? It's Elizabeth's ranch. Fancy-Josie-pants has no business selling the love of her mother's life."

"But..." Lizbet laughed again, thinking of the havoc they could cause.

Tennyson stood and stretched. *"Hmm, it's been too long since I stirred up a pot!"*

"What do you suggest?" Lizbet asked. "Because on the day of the party, I can't be anywhere near your pot-stirring."

Tennyson winked at her. *"Don't you worry. You won't be. Just leave it up to me."*

"You do know you're a cat, right? And I hate to remind you of this, but a lot of creatures don't like you."

"I know that! That's the way I like it. It does one absolutely no good to get chummy with one's lunch or snack, let alone dinner. It complicates things." Tennyson rolled onto his belly, sat up, and licked his paws. After a moment of quiet grooming, he said, *"So, while it's true a good many creatures don't want to play hopscotch with me, they will listen when I tell them how to save their homes. When an owl announces a fire in the forest, no one stops to quibble about the mouse he ate for supper. You'll see."*

Declan showed up at his mom's house on a Saturday night. He found her in the kitchen nursing a coffee while shuffling through a pile of papers full of glossy images of beautiful homes. She glanced up when he walked in, gave him a brief smile, and returned to her work.

"I want to meet my grandfather," Declan announced, leaning against the kitchen counter.

His mom's shuffling paused for a second then resumed. "I thought you understood that we should wait for him to initiate contact."

"Why?"

A scowl settled over his mom's forehead and she lifted her gaze to meet his. "A relationship with your grandfather is a tightrope act. I thought you knew that."

"I don't know my grandfather, and I'm afraid at this rate, I never will."

"Justified fear. But what I don't understand is why you feel a need to know him."

"He's my grandfather. He's half of who you are. A quarter of me."

His mom sipped her coffee, swallowed, and thought for a moment before responding. "I like to think that I am nothing like my father, and I can say with some assurance that you are nothing like him at all."

"I'd like to form my own opinion."

Gloria placed her mug on the table. "Of course I can't stop you from reaching out to him, but I have to warn you of the risks."

"Risks?"

"There's a lot of money involved. Right now, as far as I know, I'm still his sole beneficiary, but that could change in a heartbeat."

A cold, hard knot formed in Declan's throat. He tried to talk around it. "So, you don't want me to meet my aging, sick grandfather because you're afraid that I might piss him off and he'll cut you out of his will?"

"Sweetie, please don't make me into a mercenary..."

"I didn't make you a mercenary!"

Gloria hugged her papers to her chest as if to protect her heart. "It's not just the money. My father is manipulative and cold. It took me years of therapy to be free of his voice in my head. I don't want you to be hurt by him." She paused. "He's not evil. I don't want you to think he eats babies for breakfast or sells virgins to the highest bidder. He's just... He is who he is, and I am who I am. Together we're oil and water. We don't mix. He's too used to getting his way."

Declan lifted his shoulder. "Don't you think it's possible he's changed in the ten years since you last spoke with him?"

"A tiger can't change his spots."

Declan thought about pointing out that tigers have stripes, not spots, but he held his tongue. For a half second. "He's a man, not a tiger."

"Says you," Gloria said with a snort.

"People change all the time, especially when they get old and sick."

Gloria took a long breath and blew it out through her nose. "Still... there's the will."

"How do you know he hasn't changed it already?"

Gloria winked at him. "Leo Cabriolet is his attorney."

Declan knew that Godwin and Cabriolet played tennis every Tuesday at the club. He'd heard about Cabriolet, but had never met him.

"That's convenient. Isn't there lawyer-client confidentiality?"

"Don't be a pain." Gloria picked up her coffee and took a long swallow. "You know I don't like it when you get like this."

"Like what?"

"Like you're the adult. You're still a kid."

Declan blinked at his mom, trying to remember her as the fun-loving woman who had read him *Horton Hears a Who* complete with animal noises. After a moment, he gave up, rolled his eyes, and turned to leave.

"Darling," Gloria called after him.

He slowly turned.

"There's a party at the Westmoors' ranch this weekend. Would you be interested in catering?"

He'd catered numerous times at business functions for his mom in the past. The money was always good, and the work was as easy as keeping the trays full of hors d'oeuvres. "Sure."

Gloria smiled. "See? We all do what we can if the price is right."

At that, he thought about turning down the job, but the thought of escaping to Duke made him bite his lip and bang out the back door.

Lizbet was standing in the backyard singing to the chickens when the big black Mercedes pulled down

the drive. Her voice caught in her throat when the car doors opened.

"Who is it?" the chickens clucked and bobbed around her feet.

Lizbet squinted against the early morning sun and watched the passengers spill from the car. Declan, a woman in a navy pantsuit with a silky paisley scarf, and the tall dark man she'd seen earlier with Josie. She wondered at the Declan connection.

"Friend or foe?" the chicken Lizbet called Spotty wanted to know.

"I'm not sure," Lizbet said, "but I'm sure they won't hurt you or your eggs."

"But are they here to turn the ranch into a wannabe cowboy playground?" Bachman, the rooster, demanded.

"I'm not sure," Lizbet said. "I'll go and find out."

She walked slowly, because she really didn't want to meet Declan and these well-groomed people in her mud-spattered overalls, but since her curiosity matched the chickens', she straightened her shoulders, tucked her basket of seeds over her arm, and went to greet them.

Her steps faltered when Josie's familiar BMW turned down the drive. Lizbet turned and headed for the house. She sprinted up the stairs, stepped out of her farmer clothes, slipped into her favorite skirt, pulled on a lacy blouse she and Maria had picked up at the thrift store, tied her hair into a loose knot at the back of her neck, and

smeared on lip gloss. After a quick look in the mirror, she felt ready.

But she didn't know what for.

Declan's heart lifted, as it always seemed to do, the moment he saw Lizbet. She wore a black wrinkly skirt with a scattered pattern of daisies on it and a lacy white blouse. Everything about her was breezy and casual, especially in comparison to his mom's stiff business wear. He couldn't help smile. He could tell she was nervous by her doubtful eyes and the way she held her back tall and straight, and her chin high.

"So is this the girl Josie told me about?" Gloria whispered under her breath to Declan.

"I don't know. What has Josie been telling you?" Declan returned.

Gloria pressed her lips together and lowered her eyebrows as if she were concentrating on a puzzle with missing pieces rather than looking at a waiflike girl with riotous dark curls and a funky style of clothes.

Godwin, on the other hand, halted as if frozen. He stood beside the Mercedes, his expression intentionally blank as if he were betting on a losing hand in a game of poker.

Declan reached his hand for Lizbet. To his relief, she took it. He had wondered if she would. "Mom, Godwin,

this is Lizbet Westmoor. She's Elizabeth Westmoor's granddaughter."

"Daugherty's daughter," Gloria said, plastering on a fake smile. "It's lovely to meet you, finally. I've heard so much about you."

"From Josie?" Lizbet asked, sounding as if she knew that Josie wouldn't have had said anything good about her.

"And others." Gloria laughed, but it sounded harsh. "You have to admit, you have an unusual story."

Lizbet gave a small nod, acknowledging the truth of Gloria's statement. "People have been talking about me?"

"Everyone is anxious for Daugherty to get well and tell her side of things," Gloria continued, "and hopefully that will happen soon, but until then, we have only you to fill us in."

"Mom." Declan sensed Lizbet's discomfort and squeezed her hand. To his surprise, it was Godwin who came to Lizbet's rescue.

"Gloria, we don't have time for you to fill your gossip teacup. We have an event to plan," Godwin said after rousing from his momentary paralysis.

"Of course," Gloria said. "But you will come to our little get-together, won't you?"

"I wasn't planning—" Lizbet began.

"You have to come!" Gloria turned to Declan. "Tell her she has to come. Everyone will want to talk to you. It was awfully brave of you to live on that island alone."

"I didn't live alone. I lived with my mom. It was all I knew, which means it was more convenience than courage."

"But how did you manage?" Gloria pressed.

"Gloria, I know you're curious," Godwin interrupted her, "but we're on a tight schedule. And maybe Miss Westmoor doesn't want you prying into her life."

"It's okay," Lizbet said. "I don't blame her or anyone for being curious."

"So you'll come?" Gloria pressed.

Lizbet turned to Declan for answers, but he didn't offer any. "I wasn't planning on it," she said, directing her attention back to Gloria. "I wasn't sure Josie wanted me there."

"Maybe not, but everyone else will," Gloria pressed. "Say you'll come!"

"Sure."

"Fabulous!" Gloria clapped her hands together and looked as pleased as a kitten with a bowl of milk.

"Now that we have at least one confirmed guest on our RSVP list, I suggest we decide where to actually hold the event," Godwin said, taking his wife's arm and leading her to the white split-rail fence that separated the driveway from the pasture.

"You'll be coming, right?" Lizbet asked Declan.

"Yes, but not as a guest."

"What does that mean?"

As they walked along the fence, he explained to her that he would be catering the party.

"Can I do that, too?" Lizbet stooped, grabbed a handful of tall grass, and fed it to the Arabian nickering and tossing his head.

"Why would you want to?"

Lizbet stroked the horse's nose and the creature leaned toward her as if drawn by an invisible string. "I'd like to earn some money. I can't get a job because I don't have a social security card. I asked Elizabeth to help me, but with moving, she has a lot on her plate." Lizbet paused and added in a soft tone, "Either that, or else she keeps forgetting."

A small black and white goat pressed himself against the chicken wire lining the fence, trying to get closer to Lizbet.

"Is that possible?"

Lizbet nodded. "I would never want to admit that Josie might be right, but Elizabeth is... forgetful."

"In what way?"

"Little things. The teakettle left on the stove too long. The chicken pen's gate left unlatched."

A trio of robins sat on the fence inches from them, as if they, too, wanted to be close to Lizbet.

"What are you going to do?"

"What can I do?"

"I could probably get you a job at the nursery. You seem to have made a really great impression on Mr. Neal. He asks me about you almost every day. It kills him when I tell him we're just friends."

"Do you really think you could get me a job at the nursery?"

"Sure!" Declan answered much more confidently than he felt.

"That would be great." She let out a happy sigh and gave him a quick hug.

"These animals..." Declan began.

"What about them?"

"It almost seems like..."

"Like what?"

"I don't know. I can't explain it. It's like they're drawn to you. As if they love you."

She laughed. "Is that so hard to believe? That anyone could love me?"

Heat rushed to his cheeks and he hoped she wouldn't notice. "Of course not. But they're animals."

"What does that mean?"

His cheeks grew warmer. "I'm not sure."

Color rose in her cheeks. "Of course they love me. I feed them." She looked as if she wanted to say more, but she pressed her lips together for a long beat of silence. "They love me because I love them."

Reaching out, she tousled the horse's mane between his silky ears. "This is Trotter. He likes to jump, and he can gallop really fast." She bent down so that she was nose to nose with the goat.

The creature studied her with his black beady eyes.

"This is Forest. He will eat anything!" She rubbed the fur between his horns.

"Do you have names for the birds, too?" He smirked and nodded at the robins lining the fence. The birds gazed back with shifty but intelligent eyes.

"Are you mocking me?"

"No. Not at all." Declan felt chastised, as if he'd been making light of something sacred. He scrambled for a change of subject. "Do you want me to ask if you can help cater? It's easy money. The tips are usually good and I can tell my mom you need to be paid in cash."

Indecision and something else, an emotion Declan didn't know how to read, flashed across Lizbet's face. If he'd seen it on anyone else, he would have called it calculating. But since that was a characteristic he would never associate with Lizbet, he immediately dismissed it.

But later that night, as he lay in bed thinking about her, that flash in her eyes was the last thing he saw before he fell asleep.

Chapter Sixteen

On the day of the party, Lizbet tucked a basket under her arm and headed outside. Tennyson trotted beside her. She hoped to be gone before Declan arrived, but when she got to the back porch she spotted the catering tent lying in the pasture. The poles had yet to be erected and it looked like a giant white deflated balloon. The scrunch of tires on gravel announced the arrival of one white catering van as it turned down the drive. A second, followed by Declan's stepfather's giant Mercedes arrived.

With her hand on the still-open back door, Lizbet debated. She could go inside and hide out, but then it would be hard to be in contact with the animals. She needed to be somewhere close to Tennyson. Although she loved her cat, she didn't want any of the animals to get hurt in their effort to save the ranch and she knew that Tennyson placed little value on the lives of rodents, rabbits, squirrels, and... actually, anyone that wasn't a person or a cat.

Declan, wearing a pair of black pants, a silky bowtie, and a white button-down shirt, climbed out of the catering van and headed her way. He held two white aprons in his hand, and the strings fluttered around his legs.

"Hey," he said, his eyes softening as he gazed at her, "my mom said you turned down the catering job."

Lizbet nodded.

"Is it because of Josie? Did she pressure you to say no? Because if she did, I can talk to Mr. Croft. He's the caterer."

"No, it wasn't Josie."

"Then why don't you want to do it?" His eyes pleaded with her. "It'll be more fun with you there."

"I don't like large groups of people," she admitted. It was the truth, but it wasn't the whole truth. She hoped nothing in the tone of her voice would tell Declan that.

Declan's hopeful expression faded. "I guess I get that."

She hated lying to him. Placing her hand on his chest, she said, "I'll see you later."

"Wait! Where are you going?"

She nodded at the basket draped over her arm. "I'm going to pick mushrooms."

"Mushrooms? Seriously?"

"There are very few things as serious as a good mushroom."

"Okay, now I know you're lying. Are you really just going to disappear?"

"I don't want to be around when my aunt gets here. If you haven't figured it out yet, she pretty much hates me."

"That's just because she's threatened by you."

"What? Why would you say that?"

Declan sucked in a deep breath. "Her relationship with her mom isn't great, right?"

Lizbet agreed with a nod of her head.

"And suddenly you're here and she loves you. Elizabeth fell in love with you on the spot while Josie has been trying to make her mom love her for most of her life."

"Well, she hasn't been trying very hard," Lizbet said.

Declan looked over his shoulder to make sure no one could overhear them. "If she were honest with herself, she'd probably disagree with you. The trouble is, she doesn't know how to—" He cut off his words when his mom rounded the corner, her expression tense.

"Declan! There you are," Gloria said. "How are things going with Mr. Croft?"

"I'll go check," Declan said. And yet he didn't move.

"And what are you doing?" Gloria asked Lizbet with a brittle smile.

"Making myself scarce."

Gloria's scowl deepened. "It really is a shame you won't stay for the party."

"Large crowds make me nervous."

"Well, if you were my daughter, I'd tell you to buck up. You live in the real world now."

Declan elbowed his mom. "She's not your daughter."

"I just think she belong here," Gloria said, looking increasingly put out. "She shouldn't be hiding. She's Elizabeth Westmoor's granddaughter and as such—"

"Mom! You aren't one to lecture on familial bliss." Declan put his arm around his mom's shoulder and steered her to the now-billowing catering tent. He shot Lizbet an apologetic smile over his shoulder.

The tension in Lizbet's shoulders eased as she watched them walk away. She almost felt bad about what was about to happen. "I can't stay here to watch," she whispered to Tennyson. "How bad will it be?"

"It won't be bad at all. It will be glorious and gory!" the cat retorted.

"Gory?" Lizbet squeaked. "You promised me no one will get hurt!"

"Well, gory might not be the right word. How about messy?"

"Do you want to tell me what you have planned?"

The cat craned his neck to look at her. *"You don't want to know."*

Apprehension clawed in Lizbet's belly. "I've got to get as far away from here as possible."

"Finally, something we can agree on."

Lizbet whirled and came face to face with Josie. Today she had on a light gray skirt and a frilly white silk blouse. It was the most feminine thing she'd ever seen Josie wear.

"Who are you talking to?" Josie asked in a quieter voice.

"Myself." Lizbet sniffed.

"My mother tells me you've taken a job at Neal's Nursery." Josie studied her.

"Yes. Mr. Neal... We're going to work something out until I can get a social security card. He's being really kind."

Josie flushed and guilt stained her cheeks. "I don't want you to think I'm not sensitive to your situation. You obviously care a great deal for Daugherty, but I know..."

Lizbet waited, wondering what Josie would say. Finally, Josie turned away without saying anything, leaving Lizbet to wonder what Josie did or did not know.

Josie's brief moment of humanity almost made Lizbet doubt Tennyson and his schemes. But since she knew that neither Elizabeth nor hundreds of animals deserved to lose their homes, she decided to wait and see what happened. Besides, she didn't know what Tennyson had planned.

"How bad is it going to be?" she whispered to Tennyson as soon as they were in the shelter of the woods.

Tennyson lifted his tail and strutted down the path ahead of her. *"I already told you. It's not going to be bad. It'll be good. Very, very good."*

Declan watched Lizbet walk away wishing he could go with her. He went through the motions of setting up tables, chairs, spreading the white linen table cloths, and placing the flower arrangements as directed, but his thoughts kept wandering back to Lizbet.

Was he so into her because he couldn't have her? She refused to take him seriously because she thought they could still be siblings, despite his father's patent denial. A few weeks ago he would have eaten his shirt just to have Nicole smile at him and now that he and Nicole were both going to Duke—and Jason was not—he wasn't interested in Nicole anymore.

Was it possible that he only wanted what he couldn't have? What did this say about him? Declan ran a finger around his shirt collar. He wasn't used to wearing a tie and he didn't like it. It reminded him too much of a noose.

Someone in the catering van yelped.

"What is it now?" Mr. Croft barked from behind the bar. The goblets jiggled as he bobbed up and hit his head against the shelving.

"Nothing," Missy said in a trembling voice that clearly said something was wrong. She stuck her head out of the van and waved Declan over as soon as Mr. Croft ducked back behind the bar again.

Declan tried to casually stroll across the astro turf. He climbed into the van where Missy shook with distress. He liked Missy and he knew she was a talented cook. Everything she made not only tasted like it came from heaven but also looked like a work of art.

"What's the matter?" he whispered.

"My nail," she whimpered.

"Your what?"

"My nail!" She held out her hand, showing him her four long creamy fingernails embellished with daisies. One finger had a stubby plain old fleshy looking nail. "My nail fell off. It's somewhere in here." She looked ready to cry.

"By in here, you mean in the van?"

"Scary scenario—in the food."

Declan studied the platter of fresh shrimp and poked at it with his fork. Then he went to the pasta salad. Both dishes seemed like the perfect hiding place for a fake fingernail.

"What are we going to do?" Missy asked.

Declan thought about pointing out that since he had all of his fingernails intact, "we" wasn't the real pronoun she was looking for, but he just shrugged. "I guess we wait for someone to bite down on it and hope no one chokes."

"Missy! Declan!" Mr. Croft barked.

"I'm so fired," Missy moaned.

Declan patted her back. "Maybe it fell off before you got here."

Missy shook her head. "No. I know they were all here when I put on my apron. I would have noticed when I moved my ring."

Declan knew it was a standard practice for the married caterers to move their wedding rings to their right hands. It helped them get bigger tips.

"Missy! Declan!" Mr. Croft repeated. "What are you doing? It's time to get this show on the road!"

"Don't tell anyone, okay?" Missy whispered.

Declan nodded.

"I'm so fired," Missy groaned, exiting the van.

Lizbet went deeper and deeper into the woods. She'd never really taken the opportunity to explore all of Elizabeth's property before, but now, as she wandered along the path beneath the thick canopy of pines, cedars, and firs, she wondered why. The sun sent beams of sparkly light through the branches. Robins, woodpeckers, and squirrels called hello. Fragile lilies lifted their white blossoms skyward, hoping to catch the sunbeams.

A dragonfly flitted past. *"Follow me,"* he said in a voice so low, so hushed, that she thought it might have been her imagination. She did as he asked.

The light faded, despite the noon sun, as the trees' canopy grew denser. The ground sloped upward and Lizbet

scrambled up the path. The dragonfly darted in front of her, just out of reach. The hill crested and suddenly Lizbet stepped into the open air. Large stones circled the clearing. One large altar-like stone with a slab of granite stood in the center.

"What is this place?" Lizbet asked.

But no one answered.

She glanced overhead, hoping and expecting to see birds or squirrels, or anyone or anything, but the air was heavy with silence.

A thought or distant memory came back to her. Draw not nigh hither: put off thy shoes from off thy feet, for the place whereon thou standest is holy ground.

Lizbet didn't question. Even though she didn't know if the thought came from within or from without, she did as she was asked. She sank to the ground and pulled off her sandals. She crossed her legs, and placed her shoes in her lap. Her head grew heavy, and her eyes shut as a wave of fatigue swept through her. Lying on her side and using her arm as a pillow, she slept.

It started with the frogs. Small, slimy, and green, the tree frogs dropped from tent poles and landed on the bar.

"What the—hey!" The bartender used his white towel to swat at the jumping frogs.

A lady in a white sundress screamed when she opened her purse and a mouse climbed out.

A wren flew beneath the tent and beat his wings against the canopy, making the sound of jungle drums.

Declan watched his mom frantically totter from one end of the hospitality tent to the other in her three-inch heels as she waved a napkin in the air and shouted, "Shoo!"

A black and white spotted goat darted inside, jumped onto a table and began wolfing down an overweight bald man's steak. "Hey!" the man cried, pushing the goat to the floor.

The goat let out a bleat that sounded like a laugh before bounding onto another table and scarfing a bleached-blond woman's chicken breast. The woman screamed and backed away, taking down chairs in her hurry to distance herself from the creature eating her lunch.

Declan watched, his mouth dropping with amazement as squirrels, mice, and rats scampered across tables, ran over chairs, and scaled the tent poles. Throughout it all, Lizbet's giant marmalade cat sat in the corner watching. Declan swore it looked as if it were grinning. But that wasn't possible. Cats couldn't grin.

Right?

If Lizbet's cat was here, did that mean Lizbet was, too? He scanned the room, taking in the chaos, the screaming women, the flustered men, the cavorting animals. It seemed almost staged. Choreographed. Intentional.

But that was impossible.

He'd heard of lion tamers, of course, but no one he knew of trained frogs, or squirrels, or goats... and was that an opossum waddling across the Astro Turf?

A lady in a sapphire-colored sheath began to scream. She fished a finger into her mouth and pulled out an object seconds before fainting.

"What's going on?" Missy whispered as she climbed from the back of the van.

"I think Mrs. Dutton found your fingernail," Declan whispered back.

Lizbet slipped into a deep sleep. Men and women with jet black hair danced before a fire.

> *Sun of light, stars of day,*
> *Make me thine, this I pray.*
> *Meld my heart. Take my hands.*
> *May I serve in distant lands?*
> *Bless the beasts, calm the sea,*
> *Let all thy earth a witness be.*
> *Of thy bounty and thy grace.*
> *Let all of nature reflect thy face.*

Lizbet woke with a jolt. Sitting up, pushing the hair away from her face, she took stock of her surroundings. Where was she? Slowly, her memories returned. The woods. The circle of stones. Still, even as awareness flooded back, she found the quiet deafening. Where were the animals? The

breath and life of the forest? She climbed to her feet and brushed off the dust, grass, and twigs from her skirt and blouse. She spun around, wondering which direction to go in. This, she decided, must be how those who can't talk to animals feel all the time, every day.

"Hello?" she called out. "Anyone?"

Silence answered.

"Can anyone point me toward the ranch?" When she heard nothing and no one, she sat down on a rock and tried to sort things out for herself. The sun to her left. Shadows to her right. This wasn't helping. She studied the trees, but the foliage looked as full and dense at one place as another.

Standing, she decided the only thing to do was look for her own footsteps.

But where were the animals? She knew there had to be some sort of creature nearby, so why weren't they answering her? They always had before. "Hello?" she called again and got the same response.

Feeling anger spiked with a twinge of fear, she pushed into the trees and stumbled through briars and bushes that scratched her legs and caught her skirt in their branches. She disentangled herself.

Swearing, she returned to the circle of stones. What was it about this place? It was as if it didn't want her to leave because it had something it wanted her to know, something it wanted her to understand.

As she closed her eyes, memories of the strange dream floated back to her. Native Americans chanted in a tongue she'd never heard before but perfectly understood. How was that possible? And the rhyme? The words floated back to her as clearly as if she were hearing it again for the first time.

> *Sun of light, stars of day,*
> *Make me thine, this I pray.*
> *Meld my heart. Take my hands.*
> *May I serve in distant lands?*
> *Bless the beasts, calm the sea,*
> *Let all thy earth a witness be.*
> *Of thy bounty and thy grace.*
> *Let all of nature reflect thy face.*

What did it mean? Did it have anything to do with this circle of stones? The roughly hewn rock altar?

Bedlam was the word that kept coming back to Declan. Ladies screaming, men swearing, animals in all shapes and sizes overrunning the party. He barely noticed when a car pulled in the drive. Two car doors slammed. Declan turned to see Elizabeth and a painfully thin, pale woman who looked vaguely familiar standing at the edge of the pasture.

"What is going on?" Elizabeth asked, balling her hands and placing them on her hips.

The woman's lips curled into a smile. "Lizbet," she said.

And then Declan knew exactly who she was.

Daugherty.

From Declan's Research
Indigenous North American belief systems
include many sacred narratives. Such spiritual s
tories are deeply based in Nature and are
rich with the symbolism of seasons, weather, plants,
animals, earth, water, sky and fire.

Chapter Seventeen

When I get back to the ranch—if I get back to the ranch—I'll look up the indigenous people of this area on Google," Lizbet promised out loud. "I'll learn about their beliefs, the legends, and lore."

A cloud shifted in the sky and the sun touched Lizbet's skin, warming her. "I don't know what good I can do, but I can try. But first, I have to get back to the ranch. I can't stay here by myself." And at that moment, it struck her that this was exactly what she and her mother had been doing on the island. They had been stagnant, merely surviving, not interfacing with others, not learning, serving, or giving. Keeping to themselves, they'd provided the world little value. True, they hadn't hurt anyone, but they hadn't given a thing in return for the use of the world's air, the sun's warmth, and the earth's bounty.

She didn't know how she'd be able to explain this thought to her mother, or if she'd ever have the chance, but she knew she had to try. She also knew that if she wanted to belong to the world, she had to contribute something, she had to make it a better place, and she couldn't do that from where she was now.

"I need to get back," she told the sky. "And I don't know how to do that on my own."

She dropped to her knees to pray.

A sound startled her.

She looked up and met the gaze of a brown-eyed buck. He stared at her silently before turning away. She followed. She didn't try to communicate with him because words, for once, weren't necessary.

By the time Lizbet stumbled out of the woods, the sun hung low over the mountains. The party tent was once again a deflated thing on the lawn. The chairs and tables had been dismantled and stacked in the back of a pickup that had Tucker's Party Truck emblazoned on its side with a picture of a pug wearing a pointy pink and white hat.

She found Declan using a stick to pick up pieces of trash off the lawn. He brightened when he saw her.

"Go inside," he told her, smiling brightly.

"Why? How was the party?" she asked, although given the scattered food and debris, she had a pretty good idea.

Declan shook his head. "A disaster. But with a happy ending."

"What does that mean?"

"Go inside, you'll see," he said, pushing her shoulders toward the house.

Tennyson jumped out of a tree and landed with a thud beside her. She scooped him up. "Did everything go as planned?" she whispered into his fur.

"Yes and no," Tennyson purred.

"You're not going to tell me anything either?"

Tennyson wiggled out of her arms and ran toward the house. Lizbet followed.

The conversation and laughter stopped as soon as Lizbet opened the kitchen door. Seated at the table were her grandmother, her aunt, and her mother. Lizbet collapsed into her mother's open arms.

"Let me make some tea and cookies," Elizabeth said, rising. "All this catching up will take a while."

"Let me, Mother," Josie said. She stood and placed a gentle hand on her mother's shoulder, pressing her into the ladder-back chair. "You sit."

"Okay." Lizbet's mom gave a nervous laugh. "I'm not sure where to start. It's been so long. It seems like it was just yesterday that I was a girl in the kitchen, but then I see Lizbet and I know so very much has happened."

"Start at the beginning," Elizabeth coaxed.

"And then get to the end," Lizbet added, settling on a chair beside her mom. "I really want to know who tried to kill you and why."

"Okay, first off, I don't think anyone tried to kill me," Lizbet's mom said. "I'm pretty sure it was an accident."

"What? But they killed Wordsworth!" Lizbet's world shifted.

"Knowing how protective Wordsworth was, it most likely in self-defense. Here's what happened—I was arguing with Rose's ex-husband..." She broke off and blinked several times. "I guess I need to explain that, too. I have an awful lot of explaining to do. But first, I don't think Rose's ex meant to hurt me. We were arguing, yes. But I tripped, fell, and hit my head. He didn't touch me."

Elizabeth reached across the table and patted her daughter's hand. "Just start at the beginning."

"As you know, twenty years ago I went sailing with a few friends. Our boat capsized and Debbie, Kelly, and Rich made it back to shore. I did not. I washed up on Blackstone Island. Unfortunately, I couldn't remember anything—who I was, where I was from, nothing. Zip. A woman nursed me back to health. She and her daughter lived alone on the island." She paused and laid her hand over Lizbet's and gently squeezed. "That was you."

Lizbet rocked back in her chair. "I'm not your daughter?"

"Oh, you are. You absolutely are. In every single way, except for, you know, biologically. I couldn't possibly love you any more than I do now. You saved my life. I would have ended my own long ago if I hadn't had you."

"Why?" Elizabeth wailed. "You were such a happy child! And I know you were happy until the moment you stepped on that boat."

"But I couldn't remember any of that! I only knew what this woman had told me. She said my name was Rose and she claimed to be Daugherty. I don't pretend to know or understand all of her reasoning."

The teakettle whistled and Josie pulled out cups, saucers, sugar, and cream.

"I couldn't remember who I was or my previous life."

"Why didn't this Rose-Daugherty person help you?" Lizbet asked.

"That's what I want to know," Josie said. She had a cup of flour in one hand and a spatula in the other. The expression on her face made her look as if she were preparing for battle armed with kitchen weapons. "All she had to do was turn on the news or pick up a newspaper to know we were searching for you."

"We didn't have a TV, and we didn't get the paper. Daugherty... I mean, Rose, was hiding from an abusive husband. She couldn't or wouldn't risk her life to return me to mine. Besides, I know she was grateful for my company. She often said I was a gift from God."

"But after she died, why didn't you return to the mainland?" Josie asked.

"Where would I go? What would I do? What if someone tried to take Lizbet away from me? I worried every day that Daugherty's—" She paused and laughed. "I have to stop calling her that! Anyway, I worried her ex would find us and lay claim to Lizbet. I couldn't risk losing her. At least on the island we were self-sustaining. We had our garden. We had plenty of money from the sale of the blackberry wine business. Together, I thought we had everything we needed.

"On the island, I had no idea who I was. I had no one to turn to for help. I thought I was alone." She reached over and took her mom's hand. "But I'm not alone. And I'm not scared." She gave Lizbet a loving smile. "You are my daughter. You'll always be so. No one can take what we share away. Besides, we have no real way of knowing how old you are. According to Rose—who I knew as Daugherty—she disappeared before you were born about seventeen years ago." She lifted a shoulder. "We'll claim you are eighteen."

"Aren't you worried that Rose's ex will find us now?" Lizbet asked.

Rose shook her head. "I'm not afraid of him."

"This guy must know he can't have any legal claim on Lizbet, so why he did he come looking for her?" Josie asked.

"He wasn't looking for just her, he was looking for Rose."

"What happened to Rose?" Lizbet asked. A tight fist of pain clenched in her belly.

"I think she knew she was dying even before I arrived. At the end, she contacted a friend who brought out a doctor, but he said she'd left it until too late. They took her to a hospital on Whidbey Island where she died." Rose met Lizbet's gaze. "I'm so sorry. You and I were both lost for a while after that."

"But this man, Daugherty's ex, found you," Lizbet said.

Rose nodded. "He did. I don't know how. And it was just as I feared. He wanted Lizbet."

"Why?" Lizbet asked. "He doesn't even know me."

"But he knows who you are. He knows what you're capable of."

Lizbet froze.

"What's that?" Josie demanded.

"Goodness, you make it sound as if Lizbet has secret powers!" Elizabeth laughed.

"Of course she does," Rose said calmly. "We all do. Just not all of us have developed them." She picked up her teacup and winked at Lizbet over the rim before taking a sip.

With Daugherty living on the ranch, Josie was fine with Elizabeth moving back home. Daugherty still wasn't a hundred percent, but every day her health grew stronger.

About a week after her release from the hospital, Elizabeth announced it was her turn to host a party.

"Are you sure, Mother?" Josie, who had taken to spending most evenings at the ranch, asked. "Our last one bombed."

"We'll have this one on the island," Elizabeth announced.

"My island?" Daugherty asked.

"Of course. I'm sure everyone is curious to see where you've been and how you got along," Elizabeth said. "Besides, I'm proud of you. I want them all to know how amazing you are. I also want to invite Frank Forsythe and reunite him with his grandson."

"And John Lamb?" Lizbet asked, sliding her mom a knowing smile.

Daugherty blushed.

"Do you want to tell me about him, Mom?" Lizbet asked.

Daugherty opened her mouth as if to say something, but then quickly closed it. "Uh, no. I don't think I do."

Lizbet placed her hands on her hips, ready to press the matter, but Daugherty flushed and ran up the stairs. Lizbet thought about following, but decided against it. If she could keep her secrets, she guessed that her mother could keep her own, as well.

Someone knocked on the door. Lizbet answered it to find Declan leaning against a porch post, one ankle crossed over the other. "I told you so," he said with a smug smile.

She matched his grin. "You know, I'm glad."

"Yeah?" he asked, pulling away from the pillar and heading her way.

She nodded.

He reached for her with one hand and brushed her hair away from her face with the other. "Can we go somewhere?"

"Like where?" She leaned into to his hand cupping her cheek.

"Somewhere I can kiss you in a most unbrotherly sort of way."

Smiling, she slipped her hand into his. "I think I know just the place." Hand in hand, they crossed through the pasture.

"Where are you going?" Trotter wanted to know. Ever since their midnight ride to Josie's, where he'd learned that there was an entire world to be explored, he'd been eager to see new places and things.

"Somewhere for just the two of us," Lizbet said.

Declan laughed. "It's almost like you're talking to them."

"To who?" Lizbet asked, but she knew.

"The animals. That horse just nickered and you responded."

"I was talking to you," Lizbet said.

"Were not," Trotter said.

Lizbet shot the horse a dirty look, but it was hard to keep a frown on her face. She ducked under the boughs of a cedar tree and Declan followed close behind. They walked side by side on the narrow path, their shoulders occasionally bumping.

"I want to show you this amazing place," Lizbet said. "I found it on the day of the party when I left to collect mushrooms."

"You didn't find any mushrooms..."

"That's right. I found something better."

"It's hard to imagine anything better than this," Declan said, pulling her in for another kiss.

"That's good," Lizbet agreed after a few long kisses. "But I think you'll like this place. It had a reverent vibe."

"Reverent, huh?"

She shrugged. "I can't think of a better word for it."

"I'm not a reverent sort of guy," he reminded her. "I don't believe in vibes."

"Well, I think that's very silly of you. Everyone believes in vibes."

"No they don't," he said.

She liked how they could disagree without arguing. "You'll see," she said.

Only he couldn't, because she couldn't find the clearing with the circle of stones.

"So weird," she said, after wandering down one wooded path after another.

"Here," Declan said, pulling his phone out of his pocket, "let me look it up on the GPS. If it's as big as you say it is, it should show up."

Lizbet watched the phone load, but they didn't get reception. The sharp wave of disappointment surprised her. "I really wanted you to see it." Although she couldn't say why this was so important to her. She felt pressed to share it, and wanted to know if others could feel its hypnotic pull.

But then, looking into Declan's eyes, she decided he had a hypnotic pull of his very own. One that she found impossible to resist.

From Declan's Research
Be praised, my Lord, through Sister Water; she is very
useful, and humble, and precious, and pure."
—*Francis of Assisi*

Chapter Eighteen

Daugherty and Elizabeth spent days in the kitchen cooking. Josie ordered the invitations, addressed them all by hand, and mailed them to everyone who had known and loved Daugherty before her disappearance. On the day of the party, Declan went with Lizbet to the island to hang white twinkly lights and paper lanterns in the trees. While Lizbet dusted and vacuumed inside, Declan used an old push lawnmower to tackle the lawns. They took a break when their work was done and picnicked on the lawn with ice-cold lemonade and shrimp salad sandwiches.

"Are you curious about your real mom?" Declan asked.

"Deathly curious," Lizbet admitted.

"What can you remember about her?"

"Not a lot. She was small and dark, like me. She had a high-pitched laugh, and she liked to sing and whistle. I remember she told fantastic stories about fairies and wolves and creatures that lived in the deep forests... What stays with me the most is an overwhelming sadness when I think of her—which is strange, since she died when I was so young. I want to find out more about her. I want to see if I have family and what I can learn about my father."

"You should do all of that, except for the part about your dad. From what your mom said, he doesn't sound like a nice person."

Lizbet lay back on the blanket they'd spread on the lawn and gazed up at the sky. The sun skimmed the tops of the trees, letting her know that they only had a few hours until the guests would arrive.

"It's weird to think he knows who I am, but I don't know a thing about him."

"Except he wears size-fourteen boots," Declan reminded her.

She sighed and rolled over to her side and used her arm as a pillow. "It's not much of a clue."

"Your mom will recognize him when she sees him." Declan leaned back and braced himself on his elbows.

"If she sees him. If he's smart, he'll stay away from her."

"If he's smart, he'll stay away from you." Declan sat up and ran his finger down Lizbet's arm. Her skin warmed beneath his touch.

"Yeah? What would you do about it?" she asked, grinning.

Declan puffed out his chest. "I'd take him on. My feet are just as big as his!"

"Bravery can't be measured in boot size." Lizbet rolled back onto her back, turning her face to the sun and closing her eyes.

He laughed. "That's so profound. That might be one of the most profound things you've said today."

"Just today?" She opened her eyes and saw him leaning over her, his lips inches from her own.

"You're pretty profound and also really, really pretty," he murmured, moments before he kissed her.

"Lizbet! Lizbet!" A gull swooped overhead.

Lizbet pushed Declan off her and rolled away from him. Sitting up, she gazed into the sun's glare at the gull.

Declan sat up and ran his fingers through his hair. "I'm sorry, I thought..."

"It's not you," Lizbet cut him off. "I love... kissing you, but something's wrong."

"What does that mean?"

The gulls flew overhead, calling her name, their cries full of warning.

"Shh! I can't hear!"

"Hear what?" Declan said, glancing around. "I don't hear anything."

The gulls squawked out warnings.

"A man in a boat!"

"A man with a gun!"

"Follow us!"

Lizbet jumped to her feet and ran for the cove.

"Where are you going?" Declan scrambled after her.

"My mom!" Lizbet called over her shoulder. "Something's happened to my mom."

"What?" Declan caught up to her and grabbed her elbow. "You're nuts!"

She shook him off. "Let me go!"

A little white speedboat puttered into the cove. Josie waved a greeting.

"My mom! Elizabeth! Are they with you?"

The boat sputtered up to the dock and Josie threw Declan a line. "No, they're getting a ride with Declan's folks."

Declan held the rope while Josie climbed onto the dock.

"Your parents?" Lizbet's hair had come loose and her curls blew in the wind. She tried to tame it back. She tried to feel calm. Nothing could be wrong if Daugherty and Elizabeth were with Declan's parents. Maybe the gulls were mistaken, as they sometimes were.

"My mom and stepfather," Declan clarified.

Lizbet squinted at an approaching yacht and the two figures standing on the prow. She thought she spotted Declan's mother. "But isn't that your mom?"

"With my grandfather," Declan breathed, "and Elizabeth."

"Then my mom must be with your stepfather." Lizbet's heart accelerated, even as she told herself that this should be okay.

"The same man who came before!" A gull cried. *"A man of violence."*

Lizbet yanked the rope out of Declan's hands. "Tell me quick! Do you trust your stepfather?"

"I... wait, why?"

"Just tell me!" Lizbet screamed.

"Are you all right?" Josie asked, sending Declan a questioning look. "Gaylord Godwin is a highly respected businessman of impeccable—"

Lizbet huffed with impatience, turned her back on Josie, and focused on just Declan. "Tell me, do you, for any reason, think that your stepfather would hurt my mom? Could you see him shooting my dog?"

"Listen." Declan held up his hands like a traffic cop. "I hate my stepfather, but that doesn't mean—"

Lizbet jumped into the boat, climbed behind the steering wheel, and gunned the motor.

"Hey!" Josie called after her.

Declan jumped in after her. He landed in a heap near the stern. "What are you doing?" he called, raising his voice over the thrumming engine.

"Doggie!" Lizbet spotted the pod of dolphins just ahead of her. "Have you seen my mom?"

The dolphin rose from the water. *"She's with that man. Do you wish us to stop them?"*

Lizbet nodded.

"Follow us!" the dolphins called.

Declan scrambled beside her and fell into the passenger seat. "Who are you talking to?"

"Hold on!" Lizbet told him, pushing the boat faster.

"The whales! The pelicans have told the whales!" the gulls cried.

"Oh, thank you!" Lizbet called above the roaring engine.

"This is crazy." Declan gripped the side of the boat. "Lizbet, slow down. You're going to get us killed."

A line of pelicans flew overhead, calling her name.

Lizbet raised her hand in greeting. "What did the whales say?" she screamed at the birds.

"They're on it!" the lead pelican called out.

"Make sure they don't hurt my mom!"

Declan stared at her. She met his gaze, shook her head, and turned her attention back to the open sea.

A white yacht appeared on the horizon. Lizbet pushed the boat full throttle.

"You are crazy!" Declan shouted. "You are a crazy person!"

As they approached, Godwin rose, lifted a gun, and pointed it at them.

"Hold on!" Lizbet shouted. She spun the boat to the right, but not before she saw the pelicans diving toward Godwin's boat like a line of jet fighter pilots.

Godwin put his arms over his head and ducked as an enormous orca whale rose out of the water and fell with a splash that sent Godwin's boat reeling.

"My mom!" Lizbet called to the whales and dolphins churning the water like frothy butter. "Be careful of my mom!"

Another whale jumped, sending millions of water drops like shining crystals into the air. The black and white creature glistened as it arced above Godwin's boat. Lizbet sped forward, unaware she was heading directly into the whale's descent.

Splinters of wood flew through the air as the whale landed on their boat. The dolphins curved in graceful, airborne arcs, tossing passengers and gear. Empty orange life preservers flew like confetti. Declan's body cartwheeled skyward then pummeled downward. He hit the water neck-first and disappeared into the Sound.

Lizbet dove after him, willing him to surface. Debris bobbed on the water in a pool of gasoline. Pushing aside the wreckage while bullets pinged around her, she treaded water for a moment and searched the accident scene until her leg made contact with something solid. Taking a deep breath, Lizbet pushed below the surface, scanning for Declan. He floated toward the dark deep, his shoes dragging him downward. His body limp and lifeless. A small curl of blood floated around his head.

Lizbet grabbed him by the shoulders and pushed toward the surface. She rolled him over so he could breathe. Pulling Declan's body against her chest, his head lolling against her shoulder as she back-floated, she kicked violently in any direction away from Godwin and his war against the animals.

An explosion filled the air with billowing black smoke and the acrid smell of burning fuel. Even with the salt

water stinging her eyes, Lizbet saw Godwin standing on the deck. The yacht disappeared in a purple black sky. A wave tinged with fuel washed over her. She sputtered, then holding Declan as high as she could, pushed away.

Moments later, Declan's heavy weight lifted off her. She grabbed at him and fought to keep him pressed against her chest.

"Lizzy." A finger trailed across her cheek, brushing hair from her face and eyes. She blinked. Sand gritted beneath her eyelids, the sun's white light blinded her, and salt stung her cracked lips.

Someone gathered her into her arms and began to cry. Lizbet felt the shuddering body and wet tears. She closed her eyes and opened them again. "Mom?" she asked, her face pressed against her mother's dress. Lizbet's voice sounded small and raspy, and it hurt to talk and breathe.

Daugherty crushed Lizbet against her so hard she heard her heart beating. Rocking her gently, crying quietly, and murmuring, "Thank you, God, thank you."

Beside Lizbet, Declan began to cough. He propped up on his elbow and vomited a bellyful of water.

On the rocks, Elizabeth and Josie picked their way toward the beach. Concentration and concern were written on their faces as Josie carefully helped Elizabeth find toeholds on the slippery black rocks.

Another person stood on the bluff. Lizbet closed her eyes against the sun's glare, unsure of what she really saw.

Rose. Her real mother. The woman who had died years ago. She smiled as she approached, holding out her hand, leading Lizbet into darkness.

From Declan's Research
"There are more things in heaven and earth ...
than are dreamt of."
—Shakespeare, Hamlet

Chapter Nineteen

Lizbet sat curled in the club chair by the fireplace. Even though it was late spring and the weather was slowly and surely turning balmy, Elizabeth had insisted on lighting a fire and keeping Lizbet swaddled in blankets. Her mom had purchased a laptop so Lizbet could prepare for the SATs and the Washington State Exit Exam without leaving the chair. Lizbet had returned to the work of preparing for her future. And it was work. In the days following the accident, even drawing breath had become a chore, and lifting, and pushing buttons on a keyboard was an onerous task. But worth it.

Old Dr. Harker had told them the infection in Lizbet's lungs would soon clear completely. The racking fevers had already burned their course. He'd listened to her lungs with a cold stethoscope. "Breathe," he'd say, "like you were going to yodel on a mountaintop." Lizbet disliked yodeling and cold stethoscopes, but under the doctor's care her health had improved, and breathing had become less labored. Dr. Harker had been her mother's doctor. He'd told stories of her childhood accidents.

Elizabeth poked her head into the room. "Declan's here. Do you want me to tell him to come in?"

Lizbet put the laptop aside and uncurled from the chair. She felt slightly woozy when she stood and her legs wobbled, but she hadn't seen Declan since the accident and she had a lot of questions for him.

And she was sure he had questions for her, too.

He leaned against the doorframe, backlit by the late afternoon sun, as handsome as anyone she'd ever seen. It struck her that a few weeks ago, she hadn't seen very many people, but now as her world view grew and her circle of friends widened, she could say that Declan was the most handsome boy she'd ever met and she had met more than a few.

"Can we go for a walk or something?" Declan tucked his hands into his pockets, unsure.

She shot a quick glance at the swinging door that led to the kitchen before nodding. "Get my sweater out of the closet," Lizbet whispered, "and I'll see if I can find some shoes."

Stepping over Tennyson, Lizbet found a pair of boots in the basket by the front door.

Declan pulled a nubby red sweater from the closet and showed it to her.

She nodded.

He wrapped it around her shoulders while Lizbet quietly opened the door. She breathed easier when they stepped out onto the porch and closed the door with a quiet click. Lizbet sagged against Declan with relief.

"I'm free," Lizbet breathed.

He laughed without making a sound. "Hop on," he whispered, motioning for her to climb on his back.

"Where are we going?" Lizbet asked.

"Does it matter?" he said.

With her legs wrapped around his waist and her arms circling his neck, they headed across the pasture. The horses nickered greetings.

"Declan," Lizbet began, her mouth close to his ear. "Can you tell me what really happened to your stepfather?"

"Do you mean your father?"

A chill passed through Lizbet. "Do you really think...?"

"I don't know."

He set her down on the split-rail fence that separated the pasture from the woods. Lizbet shoved her hands into the sweater pockets, while Declan climbed up beside her.

"Isn't it funny how you thought we were brother and sister only to find that we might actually be stepsiblings?" he asked.

"If I'm Godwin's daughter—that's not very funny. Any word on where he might be?"

He flushed and looked away. "Do you mean has he contacted my mother? No. I hope he never does."

"She must be devastated."

The red flush staining his neck crawled to his cheeks. "I don't get her. How could she leave my dad for him?"

Lizbet didn't know what to say, so she just took his hand. "Is it okay for stepsiblings to hold hands?"

He smirked. "We'll always be connected now."

"Oh." Lizbet let that sink in. "That's good. Right?"

He smiled. "That night on the boat, how did you know?"

"Know what?"

He jumped off the fence and came to stand in front of her. "Why did you go after Godwin's yacht?"

"I just knew..."

"The voice in your head?"

"You could say that." She cocked her head at him. "Do you still not believe?"

"I believe in some things."

"Yeah? Like what?"

"Like nothing feels as good as this," he said, lowering his lips to hers.

The End

Publisher's Note

If you enjoyed Menagerie and would like to be
notified of upcoming releases, please sign up for the
author's newsletter on her blog at
kristystories.blogpsot.com.
The signup form is on the top, right hand side.

Also, we would appreciate it if you'd
help other readers enjoy it too by:
- Recommending the book to friends, readers'
groups, and discussion boards.
- If you enjoyed Menagerie, please consider leaving
a review at your favorite online venue.

Thank you!

Mélange

Book Two in the Menagerie Series

On the sort of spring evening that lasts forever, when the sun's fading into blackness stretches for hours, Declan tried to convince himself that time really could be harnessed, and the simple pleasure he found walking beside Lizbet, listening to her laugh, would last as long as they both lived. And yet his errant reminded him that bits and pieces of life could be fleeting, that nothing lasts forever, and things could change as quickly as the weather. But fortunately, at that moment, the finicky Pacific Northwest weather sported a few wispy clouds, a smattering of dim stars dotting the darkening sky, and the promise of a cool, clear night.

"Are you sure you want to wait?" Declan asked.

"What else am I going to do?" Lizbet asked. "Besides, hanging in a bookstore is one of my favorite things to do."

"I feel weird having you walk me to my grandfather's house." He glanced at her, wondering what his grandfather would think of Lizbet's curly hair, elfin features, tiny build, and bright green eyes. His mom called Lizbet a wild child, which was, given her strange upbringing, an apt description. "It's supposed to go the other way, right?"

"What do you mean?" Lizbet turned to him.

He wanted to kiss her, but after a quick glance at his grandfather's imposing brick mansion on the other side of the long stretch of lawn, he tucked his hands in his pockets to stop himself from reaching out to her. "I'm the guy," he said. "I'm supposed to walk you home."

"But neither of us are going home. I'm going to the bookstore, and you're stalling."

"I'm not stalling."

She placed her hands on his chest to keep him away. "Yes, you are. We've been walking down this street at turtle speed..."

He wrapped his hands around her wrists, holding her close. "He's going to think I'm hitting him up for money."

"Why do you think that?"

Declan sucked in a breath. "He's going to ask about college. So, I'll have to tell him about Duke, and that will lead to a conversation about money."

"I'd rather talk about money than your stepfather."

"True that."

"But you're not your stepfather, and you don't have to talk about money. You can steer the conversation in any direction you wish."

A rustling in the bushes caught and held Declan's attention. The giant rhododendrons bordering the lawn shivered before falling still.

Lizbet followed his gaze, her expression curious and baffled.

"Probably a cat," Declan said.

Lizbet shook herself and tucked her hands into her sweater pockets. "I don't think so... it would have been a really big cat."

"A dog then," Declan said, dismissing it. "Are you going to be okay walking to the bookstore?"

Lizbet smirked. "I don't know... this is a pretty sketchy neighborhood." She waved at the turn of the last century mansions, the tree-lined street, and manicured lawns before taking his hand in hers and squeezing it. "This is the kind thing to do. Remember, this is for him, not you. I'll be fine and so will you. And more importantly, so will your grandfather."

But Declan knew that wasn't true. The whole reason he stood on the street outside his grandfather's house was because the old man wasn't fine. His days were numbered. According to his nurse, Frank Forsythe only continued to live because he was too ornery to die.

"He scares me," Declan admitted.

"I think you could take him on," Lizbet said with a grin.

"Physically, but probably not intellectually."

"If he tries to play chess, just run." Lizbet put her hands on Declan's shoulders and turned him so he faced the front gate.

"That would be cowardly..." Declan shuffled his feet.

Lizbet gave his back a gentle push.

The bushes shook again, and this time Declan caught sight of an enormous gray tail beating the bright red flowers before disappearing into the shrubs. "That's a huge dog."

"I'm not scared of a dog," Lizbet assured him.

"What if my grandfather gets to talking and I can't get away before the bookstore closes. I can't leave you here in the dark by yourself while a giant dog runs loose, terrorizing the neighborhood." Declan balked at the black wrought iron gate that separated his grandfather's house from the rest of the world.

"For one thing, no one is terrorized. And another, this is the Pacific Northwest. It's June, the longest day of the year is only a few weeks away. We have another two hours, at least, of daylight. And if your grandfather gets extra chatty, I'll take a bus home." She reached around him and pushed open the gate. "Now, march up to that door and act chummy. He's old, he's sick, and he wants to meet you."

Declan nodded and after a quick backward glance at Lizbet, the girl who had become the center of his world and his personal voice of reason in just a few weeks, he headed up the walkway.

As much as the bookstore tempted Lizbet, curiosity made her pause at the edge of Frank Forsythe's property near the now-still rhododendrons. Cocking her head, she listened for the dog who belonged to the great furry tail she'd spotted earlier. She shot Declan a quick glance. He stood on the porch with his hands shoved into his pockets, his back to her.

"Hello?" Lizbet whispered into the bushes. Silence. She gazed up at the trees lining the property expecting to catch the attention of a squirrel or even a bird, but couldn't find a creature in sight. A chill crawled down her back. "Hello?" she called a smidge louder.

The bushes rustled again and Lizbet searched for the cause. A rabbit, a chipmunk, even a skunk—there had to be an animal around. Why wasn't anyone responding? She shot the house another glance, but Declan had disappeared from the porch.

She hadn't heard the front door open, but that must have been what had happened. The nurse, Teddy, had been expecting him. Lizbet let out a little sigh of relief, pulled her sweater a bit tighter around her, and headed for the Blarney Bookstore.

The University District was an eclectic mix of shops catering to the UW's students and the historic homes of the professors and Seattle's business professionals. Lizbet's

sandals made a flopping sound as she walked and she told herself that the eerie echo wasn't in any way sinister. But goosebumps rose on her skin as she scanned the yards, trees, and shrubbery for signs of life.

Where was everyone?

When only silence answered the door, Declan stepped off the porch to peek in the window. He'd never been inside his grandfather's house so he didn't know what to expect. The tapestry rugs, wingback chairs, and oil pastoral paintings didn't surprise him. The overturned table, shattered vase, and strewn flowers across the wood floor did. He rapped on the window. Just like when he'd knocked on the door, no one answered.

He cast another glance at Lizbet. She stood at the intersection at the end of the street. Should he call out to her? What if someone had broken into his grandfather's home? What if that someone was still in the house? The further away Lizbet was, the safer she was. Squaring his shoulders and refusing to jump to conclusions, Declan jogged toward the back of the house. A shoulder-high brick wall enclosed backyard. When he couldn't find a gate, he scrambled over it and landed hard on his feet. His breath accelerated as he picked up his pace. A quick glance in the windows told him the living and dining room were

both empty. A motion-censored light flicked on when he reached the patio. Everything in the backyard screamed quiet and peaceful elegance. It was hard to imagine his grandfather had met any violence. The windows were intact, but the back door hung ajar.

Declan reached in his pocket and fingered his phone, debating on whether or not he should call the police. He poked his head through the door. The kitchen with its tall white cabinetry, scrubbed oak table, and gleaming stainless steel appliances looked like it belonged in a magazine. But a large butcher knife lay on the floor surrounded by a smattering of... what *was* that?

Declan pushed inside for a better look, then, with trembling fingers he called his mom.

Lizbet finally spotted an owl perched on the branches of a giant maple tree. It was early for an owl, but that was only one of things out of place on this strange night.

Lizbet glanced up and down the street, making sure she and the owl were alone. "Where is everyone?" she asked.

The owl swiveled his head in her direction and blinked at her. *"The wolves are back,"* he said with a hoot as if this should answer all her questions.

"The wolves? In the University District?" Her mind tripped back to the large gray tail she'd spotted in Frank Forsythe's rhododendron. Why would there be wolves

close the city center? Wolves belonged in the woods or near pastures where the slow and easy prey lived.

The owl blinked again and nodded.

"All the animals have disappeared because of the wolves?" Lizbet pressed.

"I suggest you do the same."

"Why are you here?"

"I am a sentinel. We owls have always been so."

"Admirable," Lizbet murmured. She pressed her mouth closed when an elderly couple walking a standard poodle appeared at the end of the street. She watched as the poodle sat down and refused to budge. The woman tugged on the leash and reprimanded the stubborn dog. After a moment, the man took possession of the leash, but the dog remained obstinate. The man pulled on the leash, but the poodle sat on his haunches while his collar threatened to pop off his furry head.

She turned back to the owl. "Do you know where the wolves are now?"

The owl lifted one wing and pointed at the Forsythe house.

Lizbet ran and her sandals slapped the sidewalk.

She stopped short when a giant gray wolf appeared on the sidewalk. "What... who are you?" She confronted the wolf.

He didn't answer but stared at her with blazing yellow eyes.

It occurred to Lizbet that he was trying to scare her. She balled her fists and planted them on her hips. "Answer

me!" She raised her voice and tried to infuse it with authority. "Who are you and what do you want?"

The creature flicked his tail before turning and sauntering into the dark night.

Lizbet went to the front porch and rapped on the door.

Declan answered, his face pale. Silently, he widened the door to let her in. "I thought you were the police." His voice wavered.

"Why? What happened?"

Declan nodded over his shoulder. A newscaster's voice floated through the open door, and the light flickered from a TV screen.

Lizbet started for the room, but Declan put a warning hand on her arm stopping her. "Don't," he said.

"Why?"

"Well, for one thing, I vomited in there. And another..."

"Your grandfather?"

"And Teddy, his nurse."

"Are they dead?" Lizbet whispered, although she didn't know why.

"It's... grizzly."

Lizbet put her fingers to her lips, because she knew it wasn't grizzly—not like a bear—but wolfish...

...Like a giant gray wolf.

Indie Artist Press | Brackettville, Texas